DRAGON RISING

LINSEY HALL

For Mouse.

1

Some people like to go to the movies for their first date. Or on a picnic. Maybe even a walk in the park.

Not me.

I preferred a good old demon hunt. *Then* maybe a nice dinner, followed by an icy martini with three olives.

Fortunately, Declan was my kind of guy.

And our first date was going smashingly. In both the sense that it was going well, and that the demon we were hunting was trying to smash things.

Declan and I had started our hunt in Magic's Bend. He was after a Liatora demon on behalf of the High Court of the Angels. I'd agreed to help him out in exchange for a bit of the demon's very valuable blood. And also because it was fun.

Even more, I'd promised not to kill the demon out from under him.

Apparently, I *really* liked him.

Except, Liatora demons had both wings and telekinesis, which made this bastard super dangerous in the city. We'd managed to chase him to the cliffs outside of town, thereby getting him away from people and property.

I stood near the edge of the cliff that plunged down into the sea. Waves crashed below and wind tore at my hair as I watched Declan and the demon. They flew above me, about forty feet in the air, their massive wings casting shade on the ground.

The demon was nearly twice as big as Declan, with pale yellow skin and orange eyes. His wings were a burnished red color, each one edged with serrated feathers. Knife-like claws tipped his fingers, each one twelve inches long, and his fangs gleamed in the late afternoon light.

It was rare that one of these guys escaped the underworld, and he'd headed directly for Magic's Bend, no doubt determined to eat as many people as he could. If I'd stuck around home long enough, the Council of Demon Slayers probably would have called on me to come hunt this guy, too.

As it was, I'd already joined Declan in the fight.

I gripped my mace and positioned myself, waving my hand to give Declan the signal that I was ready. He spotted me, and nodded, then dived for the demon, shooting a bolt of lightning right at him.

The electric bolt struck the demon, pushing him toward the ground. He laughed as if the lightning didn't bother him a bit.

We hadn't expected it to kill him.

Declan struck again, the lightning pushing the demon closer to me. The monster wasn't even bothering to look at the ground. Idiot didn't consider me a threat.

I began to swing my mace, working up some momentum. I'd need some serious power to knock this guy out of the air.

Declan struck a third time, and the demon tumbled lower. He flared his claws out, ready to charge Declan.

But it was too late.

I swung my mace hard, aiming for his middle. I wanted to go for the head, but that shot was harder to make. And it might kill him.

Though that was tempting, I'd made a promise.

I liked Declan enough to keep my promises to him.

The spiked ball of the mace crashed into the demon's side, and he roared, the sound vibrating in my chest. The force of the blow slammed him to the ground, and he bounced.

I yanked my chain back, determined to strike again. The demon scrambled upright, turning to face me. Rage twisted his features, and his horns turned a dark black.

Declan shot down from the sky, his hand alight with heavenly fire. He hurled the blast of flame at the demon, but the monster dodged, raising its claws and making a swiping motion.

His telekinesis picked up a nearby rock, which hurtled toward me. I dived left, narrowly avoiding a hit to the stomach with a two-hundred-pound boulder. Grass skidded under me, and I flipped up my hood, igniting the magic in my ghost suit.

The demon growled his displeasure when I turned invisible, then bellowed when Declan's fireball hit him straight in the stomach. He went flying back, his clothes alight.

I charged, swinging my mace to get it up to speed. The monster rolled on the grass, trying to put out the flames. They were slow to dissipate—heavenly fire was a pain like that—but eventually he managed. Horrible burns covered his middle, and he roared with frustration and pain.

Right before I reached him, he shot back into the sky, out of reach.

"Damn it." I yanked my hood off so Declan could see me.

We'd agreed not to use too much heavenly fire for fear of killing the demon. As much as I might have liked that, Declan was supposed to bring him to the High Court for questioning. He was currently trying to improve his reputation with the angels after our recent theft from the Heavenly Archives, and I was determined to help him.

Since his lightning couldn't hurt the demon enough and his

heavenly fire would outright kill him, we'd settled on a compromise.

Me and my mace.

"No killing," I muttered to myself. I was a creature of habit, so the reminders helped.

Thirty feet above me, the demon charged for Declan, his claws outstretched. The angel dodged, narrowly avoiding a killing blow to the chest. Faint red stripes appeared on his shirt.

Damn it.

I scowled at the demon, who looked down at me. A moment later, he flicked his wrist, and another huge rock lifted off the ground and shot in my direction. Three hundred pounds of granite headed straight for my face.

I dived low, taking a hit to the arm that made me wince. The boulder had barely glanced the edge of my arm, but three hundred pounds of granite going fifty miles an hour hurt like hell.

Thank fates it wasn't my mace arm.

I surged upright as lightning struck.

Declan was driving the demon back toward me.

Unfortunately, the demon had figured it out. He was more careful than he had been, not allowing the lightning to drive him as far down. Quickly, I inspected my surroundings. The wind whipped across the landscape, making trees shake and the sea roar.

To my left, there was a huge outcropping of rocks. It was behind the demon, so he couldn't see it.

Perfect.

I sprinted toward it, waving at Declan, who faced me on the other side of the demon. I caught his attention, and he nodded almost imperceptibly.

Thunder crashed as Declan used his lightning to drive the demon toward the rocks. I sprinted up them, leaping from boulder to boulder until I was about twelve feet in the air. I swung my mace, eying the demon as the lightning smashed into him, driving him lower.

When he was in range, I swung my mace toward his middle. I made sure to hit him harder this time—a hell of a lot harder. The metal ball slammed into him, and he plowed into the ground once again.

Before the demon could rise, Declan flew down toward him and landed on top of him, smashing the hilt of a dagger so hard into his skull that I swore I heard a crack.

The demon slumped, unconscious.

I stashed my mace in the ether and raced for them.

Declan folded his midnight wings back into his body and drew a pair of magic-dampening cuffs from the ether. He shackled the unconscious demon at the ankles and wrists, then turned to me, a grin on his face.

Damn, he looked good like this, all wind tousled and tough. With his dark hair and eyes and his chiseled features, he looked exactly like the fallen angel he was.

It turned out I was a sucker for fallen angels. At least, fallen angels named Declan. The only other one I knew was a real bastard.

I shoved the thought of Acius away. He was a problem for another time.

"Nicely done." Declan rose, dusting off his hands on his pants. "That last hit was impressive."

I shrugged. "What can I say? I'm good at what I do."

His grin widened, and he pulled me close and pressed a kiss to my lips. He drew back and looked down at me. "We make a good team."

And that was the key to a proper relationship. You worked the demon killing *into* your romantic get-togethers. That way, you could enjoy each other but not fall behind on your work. Stress was a primary killer of relationships, after all.

Mentally, I patted myself on the back for being so good at this relationship thing.

It might be my first real one in, well...forever. But I was handling it nicely. Declan made it worth it. I'd been resistant at first—trust issues were a bitch—but I was falling hard for him. And fast.

Declan gestured to the demon. "He's all yours."

This was normally the part where I'd slice his head off, but I ignored that urge. I owed Declan one for helping me break into the Heavenly Archives. His actions—against his own best interests, in fact—had saved my life.

So it was up to me to help repair his reputation with the angels. Bringing in some important bounties would help with that. Eventually, we could go Dutch on these dates. Sometimes he'd get the demon. Sometimes I would.

For now, all I was getting was a bit of blood for my sorcery. And frankly, from a demon as powerful as this one, that was nothing to scoff at.

Quickly, I drew a vial from my pocket and knelt by the demon's side. He groaned, struggling toward consciousness. His orange eyes popped open, and he looked at me, confusion on his face.

"Your magic," he rumbled. "It's...strange. So powerful. So mixed." A frown stretched across his face. "You're a Dragon Bl—"

My heart lurched, and I slammed my fist into the side of his head, knocking him unconscious again. Pain surged through my knuckles, and I shook my hand.

I glanced up at Declan.

He frowned down at me. "He could sense you."

"It's what I've been afraid of all these years." Cold dread

spread through every inch of my body. "I've created too much new magic, and my signature has grown so much that others can tell what I am—if they know what a Dragon Blood is."

"This guy did."

"Some demons do. They keep track of the most dangerous supernaturals." I chewed my lip. "This is bad."

"You need to practice controlling it."

"I know. And I have been. I just don't know if it's possible to get a rein on all of it. There's so much."

He knelt down and touched my shoulder, meeting my eyes. "Anything is possible. Especially if you're doing it."

I drew strength from his words, but it wasn't enough to squash all the worry. Acius had sensed what I was, too. I was reaching the end of the line. I'd created so much magic that my secret would be out of the bag soon.

No way I could create any more.

I shook the thought away.

The mace had left an ugly wound in the demon's side. It dripped blood, and I pressed the vial up to the wound, collecting as much of it as I could. Carefully, I recapped the vial, then wiped it off on his clothes to remove any of the red liquid that might have touched the outside. I did *not* want to get that on my skin. Not before I knew exactly what it could do.

I tucked the vial into my pocket and stood. Declan approached the demon. I expected him to take out his cuffs, but instead, he gestured to me. "Would you do the honors?"

Surprise flickered through me. "Wait, what?"

"If he knows what you are, I can hardly take him into the High Court of the Angels. And if you kill him, he's dead forever, since you're a slayer."

Warmth spread through me.

Declan is protecting me.

I was going to fall for him in no time flat, and the idea scared me. Excited me.

"Thanks." I drew my sword and turned to the demon, then sliced his head off.

Blood spurted from the neck, but the whole thing would disappear in seconds, gone forever.

Declan took my hand. "What do you say we get to the last part of our date? We could even practice you controlling your signature."

"I'd say it's the best idea I've heard all day."

It didn't take long to get back to my place. On the way, I practiced drawing my magical signature back into myself. It was like the light given off by a hundred-watt bulb, but I couldn't put a shade over it so it didn't blind people.

I was good at controlling the signature of the magic I already had, but this new magic...

It was another thing entirely.

"It's not working," I said. "I can't seem to repress it."

"You're having trouble controlling the signature now," Declan said. "But that doesn't mean you won't be able to in the future."

Fates, I hoped he was right.

But could I really?

I was terrified that it just wasn't possible.

Hell, it wasn't just that I was afraid of a future where I couldn't control my signature, and I was found out for what I was. I was afraid of the magic itself. Of what it meant about me.

I'd feared it all my life, and suddenly I was creating powers left and right.

Of course it freaked me out.

I just had no idea how to fight it. Normally I killed the things that scared me. Like, literally smashed my mace into their heads until they were dead.

I couldn't smash a mace into this.

How did one solve a problem that didn't involve maces and smashing? I had no freaking clue.

"I hope you're right." I shook my head. "But there's one thing I know—no way in hell am I making more magic. I just can't afford it."

The only problem was—could I defeat Acius if I *didn't* make more magic?

Possibly not.

I shivered, forcing the thought away. I'd face what came at me. We'd stop him.

For now, Declan and I were trying to steal two hours for a date. That wasn't too much to ask. And I wanted to get cleaned up and change into nicer clothes. Declan had the same thing in mind. He'd stashed some clothes at my place for just this reason.

As I stepped through the doorway and into the main foyer, Wally waited on the stairs. His smoky fur wafted around his form, and flames flickered in his eyes as he watched us.

Nice date?

"Spectacular." Mostly. "And it's not done yet."

I can't believe you didn't invite me.

"Um—"

A shrieking alarm interrupted my words. Red smoke drifted over the ceiling.

"Shit." I looked at Declan. "That's the council. I have to go answer it."

It was weird to just *say* it out loud. For so long, I'd hidden that part of myself. But now, Declan knew. There was no point in pretending the alarm was anything other than it was. I'd already decided I trusted him with my Dragon Blood secret. This was no different.

I was almost willing to let him come down to the sacred pool to see what the fuss was all about, but Agatha wouldn't appreciate that. Our contact with the Council of Demon Slayers was quite clear about secrecy. The agency distinctly preferred it.

"I'll go get cleaned up," he said. "You go save the world. Come get me if I can help."

"Thanks." It was nice to have a guy who respected my work.

Declan headed to my apartment, and I raced to the workshop that hid entrance to the secret cavern below our townhouse. Mari met me there, her hair only partially done up in its signature bouffant. She wore her trademark black eye makeup and the plunging dress that made her look like Elvira.

"Another red alert?" she asked, exasperated. "Shit is really hitting the fan, isn't it?"

"Seriously." Unease tugged at me.

Could it be Acius?

The fallen angel had been silent for the last week. That was the longest I'd gone without dealing with a problem he'd caused. It was only rational to think that he was in the planning stages of something big.

"Let's do this." Mari sliced her finger and held it over the corner of the table.

I joined her.

Together, we went through the steps of opening up the secret trapdoor beneath the big table. A drop of our blood moved the heavy wooden piece of furniture, and another opened the door. We raced down the spiral stone staircase, heading deep into the earth.

It took only seconds to get past the Aerlig Vines and the Lights of Truth, and soon we were in the cavern that glowed with a faint blue light from the sacred pool.

Fortunately, it had returned to full strength after Acius's demons had attacked it last week. Magic pulsed from the surface of the water, and we hurried to it.

I kicked off my boots and socks and stepped barefoot into the water. Mari did the same. A chill raced over me. Magic swirled in the air.

I reached for Mari's hand, and together, we chanted, "Here we be, let us see."

Glittering magic swirled, the blue light moving faster and faster. It shined so brightly that it nearly blinded me, then the air popped, and the magic disappeared.

An ethereal figure rose from the middle of the pool. Agatha looked like a cross between a ghost and a person. She was a rare type of ghost who could travel though the Well of Power, and she was always the one to deliver our assignments.

"Agatha." I searched her expressionless face for any clues. "What's wrong? Why the red alert?"

Please don't say Acius.

I knew I'd have to face him again—no way a monster as awful as him would just disappear and leave me alone—but I'd prefer it if he just died quietly in his sleep. Or horribly. I didn't care how he went, just that he did.

"You must come with me." Agatha's voice vibrated with power and trembled with a hint of nerves.

"Wait, what?" Mari asked.

I frowned at Agatha.

We *never* went with her. She was here so we didn't have to visit headquarters.

"The problem is more than I can explain. You must come with me to the council."

Shit. I hadn't been expecting this. But there was no arguing. Not with the command, and especially not since she sounded so freaked out about it.

"Let me grab my boots." I let go of Mari's hand and hurried out of the water, snagging both of our shoes. Since Mari had still been getting ready for the day—she was a late riser—she'd worn her black slippers down here.

Not what she wanted to wear to headquarters, I was sure, but there was no time to get anything else.

I joined her in the water and handed her the shoes, then looked at Agatha. Normally I'd crack jokes at her, but it was clearly not the time. "We're ready."

"As we'll ever be." Mari's tone was wry.

"Come." Agatha held out her spectral blue hands, and we approached, walking slowly through the crystal blue water.

I was about knee deep by the time I reached her.

Mari and I gripped her hands, and the ether sucked us in, dragging us down through the water and spinning us through space, finally thrusting us up through a pale blue pond that sat in the middle of a rolling landscape somewhere in Europe.

Neither of us knew exactly where council headquarters were located. None of the slayers did. It was a security protocol, and a good one.

The sun was setting behind the mountains here, and a chill was biting at the air. Agatha—now slightly more corporeal—turned to walk toward the old manor house that served as headquarters.

"I've never seen you look so solid before," I said as we trudged out of the sacred pool. I could tell that Agatha was somewhere in her seventies, with a serious face and neat, short hair.

"When I am close to headquarters, I have a stronger form." She stepped out of the water and onto the grass, drifting toward the manor house. "Now come. The council wishes to see you."

Mari and I tugged on our shoes, then hurried after her

toward the house. We stuck side by side, and Mari grumbled about her slippers as she pinned back the rest of her hair.

"How does it look?" she asked.

I inspected her. "Good enough."

"What does that mean?"

"Not great, but not insane." There were a few pieces hanging out, but if you were generous, it looked intentional.

"I'll take it."

Agatha stopped abruptly about fifty feet from the house. I mimicked her movements, my heart starting to pound.

I remembered this bit.

The council was very good with protective charms. They had to be.

Agatha glanced back at us. "Think of why you're here."

As soon as Agatha spoke, a wall of flame burst to life in front of us. Twenty feet tall and totally impenetrable, it blazed with ferocious heat.

I swallowed hard, staring at the flames that would soon envelop me.

2

I CRINGED BACKWARD AS THE FLAMES WARMED MY FACE, THEN forced myself to clear my mind.

I am here to help the council. I have only good intentions.

I repeated the mantra to myself as Agatha stepped through the flames, her blue form disappearing into the flickering red and orange. I drew in a steady breath, careful not to cease my internal chanting, then stepped into the flames behind her.

For the briefest moment, it hurt like hell. I nearly went to my knees at the blazing pain that licked at my skin. Then the magic sparkled, the protection charm seeping inside my mind and soul to read the truth of my intentions.

If I really *was* here to help the council, the flames would be able to sense that, and I would be fine. They'd die down, and I would be able to walk through. If I wasn't...

I'd make grilled chicken look alive.

When the pain faded enough that I could walk, I hurried through the flickering orange tongues of fire. They died down as I walked, until, finally, I was on the other side. Mari joined me a moment later.

"Fates, this place sucks," she muttered.

"Seconded." I loved my job and believed in the mission, but, holy fates, did I agree with her.

"Hurry now," Agatha said.

I strode along behind her, nerves prickling my skin as I wondered what we were here to learn.

"In all the years we've been with the council, we've never been called in at the last minute," I murmured to Mari. "We came for our annual review six months ago, so it has to be an emergency."

"Do you think it's Acius?" Worry sounded in her voice.

He'd kidnapped her a week ago while she'd been weakened by poison. Mari was as scared of him as I was, and rightly so.

"Maybe." I swallowed hard, shoving aside the nerves. "Hell, I kind of want it to be about him. We've been looking for him with no luck."

"That's the sister I know and love."

Agatha stopped about ten feet in front of the front door, and we joined her. She waved her hand over the ground, and grass and dirt disappeared, forming a deep chasm in the earth.

Smoke billowed up, as if the fires of hell were welcoming us.

"You know the drill," Agatha said.

Indeed, I did, and I hated it almost more than the fire.

Once again, I cleared my mind and filled it with my intentions. *I am here to help the council. I mean no harm.*

It didn't matter how many times I did it—it still made me ill to think of it. What if the charm was faulty?

I avoided looking down at the chasm as I stepped out over open space. My heart thundered in my chest as my foot met open air.

I fell, plummeting into the chasm. My stomach jumped into my throat as I held on to the mantra in my head.

Suddenly, my feet landed on a firm surface. I stumbled, righting myself, and opened my eyes, already knowing what I would see.

The heavy wooden door to the manor house swung open. I'd passed the test, and the enchantment had delivered me to the front step. Mari appeared next to me a moment later.

Agatha didn't, but she usually ditched us at this point. We liked to joke that she went into the chasm to visit her boyfriend, Satan. But now wasn't the time for jokes.

Together, we hurried into headquarters. The entry foyer was manned by a butler named Tony.

He was the oldest guy I'd ever seen—well over six hundred —and looked it. Surprisingly spry, though.

Tony, with his wild white hair and neatly pressed black suit, gestured to the door beyond the foyer. "They are waiting, madams."

"Thanks, Tony." I strode past him. "Say hi to the missus, for us."

"I will, madame."

We entered the huge, ornate library that served as the meeting place for the council. The arched ceiling was intricately carved and covered with gold leaves. The books that filled the shelves were rarely read, as far as I knew, but the staff carefully oiled the spines every year to keep them in good shape.

A U-shaped table filled the space. The nine council members each sat in a perfectly positioned chair—order was the name of the game here at the council—and I nearly stutter-stepped.

I'd never seen all nine before.

At most, three of them would preside over our annual reviews. But there were nine cloaked figures seated around the table. Their faces were obscured by cloaks—I'd never actually seen a council member's face besides the one who had rescued us from Grimrealm when we were kids—but I could feel their magical signatures.

Each was immensely powerful, and unquestionably good. They had the pure signatures of those whose life mission was to help the world. They inspired feelings of comfort, kindness, respect, and compassion.

It was what allowed me to trust them even though I'd never seen their faces. Honestly, it was almost like looking into their souls.

"Aerdeca. Mordaca." The figure in the middle stood. Rose. I recognized her by her voice as much as her signature. She was the one to preside over our annual reviews the most often, and I liked her the best. "Thank you for coming so quickly."

"Of course. What's gone wrong?"

"We have a problem." She looked around the table at the rest of the council members, and they all nodded gravely. "There are two things that we must show you. Things that Agatha could not."

I stepped forward into the open space between the U-shaped table. "What is it?"

"First, the seer."

Ah, shit. A seer. That was never good.

Rose tapped a bell on the table in front of her, and a clear, piercing tone rang out. A hidden door opened behind her, the wall of books swinging outward to permit a young man to enter. He had the ageless look of someone who had lived a long time but never grew older physically. It was a weird, almost CG effect.

"Kerrin here will show you what is going to come to pass," Rose said.

Mari and I shared a look. No doubt we'd be expected to stop whatever it was.

Kerrin walked around the table and stopped behind us. We turned to face him.

"The elders of the council requested that I look into the future of Magic's Bend," he said. "And this is what I saw."

I held my breath as he raised his hands. Magic surged on the air.

A vision formed in front of us, images coalescing to form a scene of unimaginable horror. An enormous serpent rampaged through Magic's Bend. The huge snake was hundreds of feet long, with fangs as long as I was tall.

I stumbled back, watching as it destroyed two buildings in the Historic District. Just like that, Mad Mordecai's and the Tasty Turtle were gone, crushed under the weight of the serpentine body that gleamed with bright green scales.

The scene shifted, showing utter destruction. Parts of the town were in ruins, smoke rising from collapsed buildings. Acius, the fallen angel with the ash-tipped wings, stood on the roof of one of the buildings on Factory Row, surveying the destruction.

"When?" The words came out on a rasp. "When does he do this?"

"Three days hence," Kerrin said. "The Great Serpent will rise, and Magic's Bend will fall."

I studied the scene, confused. "But he wants Magic's Bend for his own. Why would he do this?"

"He wants something else more," Rose said, her voice heavy with meaning.

I turned to look at her, my stomach dropping. "Me."

She nodded. "We believe so, yes."

I recalled my last meeting with him, just a week ago. I thought I might defeat him there, at his headquarters in Grimrealm. We'd had him and his minions cornered.

He'd figured out that I was a Dragon Blood—and realized that he wanted me in his collection more than anything—but I thought I'd stopped him.

I hadn't.

He'd hit me with a blast of electrical energy that had thrown me back, and my dagger had fallen uselessly to the floor. Moments later, he'd crashed through the stained glass window and flown away, bringing the last of his living cult members with him.

Now this.

I looked back toward the vision, which was as horrible as I'd remembered. Kerrin dropped his hands, and the sight faded.

"How did you think to look for this vision?" Mari asked. "Did you get an alert from somewhere?"

"We did."

I didn't like the tone of Rose's voice. She hesitated before dropping her bomb.

"Acius sent a message."

"What?" Mari snapped.

I just blinked at Rose. "Why the hell would he do that?"

"He can tell you himself." Rose turned back to the table as the words ricocheted around in my head.

Was he *here*?

No, impossible. Otherwise we wouldn't have this horrible future ahead of us. We'd have imprisoned him—killed him, more like—and stopped it from ever happening.

Rose picked something up off of the table and turned back, holding the silver circlet flat in her palm.

"Is it a holocharm?" I asked.

"It is indeed. We received it just thirty minutes ago." She set it on the ground and stepped back.

Magic flared to life. It swirled in the air, shades of gray and black mist that finally coalesced to form an image. It was as if Acius himself were standing there, tall and sinister-looking. His clothing was sleek and black, his midnight wings tipped with ash. Shadows hung heavy under his eyes, and his cheeks were gaunt. The sallow cast to his skin suggested that he wasn't well, but with my luck lately, it was just an indicator that he was tired from making progress on his evil plan.

"This message is for Aerdeca and Mordaca, the witches that I seek."

He didn't say *the Dragon Bloods.* He was hiding it, no doubt so he could use it as a tool to control us. *Do what I want and I won't turn you in.*

Well, hell no.

Acius paused for a moment, probably expecting the Council of Demon Slayers to run off and collect me. Which, they had.

When he began speaking again, it felt as if he were looking directly at me and Mari.

"Aerdeca. This message is for you. A warning, if you will. Soon, a great tragedy will befall Magic's Bend. Destruction like you've never seen."

I might have thought he was bluffing if I hadn't seen Kerrin's vision of the future.

"You know that I want Magic's Bend for my own. But now, I have something I want more. You. If you turn yourself over prior to the destruction of Magic's Bend—say, in three days' time—I will not hurt the city."

I scoffed.

If he had control of me, he could do way worse than raising a huge monster to destroy our town. That would be just the appetizer. He could make me kill everyone in Magic's Bend, and then he'd have what he'd wanted all along.

"You can meet me in the center of town, three days from now, at noon. Else your town will be destroyed. *All of it.*"

He meant the buildings as well as the people. Which, honestly, wasn't that much worse.

The magic in the holocharm died, and he disappeared.

I frowned and looked at the council. "What do we know about that snake? Where is it from?"

"We believe it is the Great Serpent, a creature of myth and legend," Rose said. "It appears in many different cultures, but the truth of the Great Serpent is that it lies asleep under the earth, waiting to be awoken."

"And that bastard is going to wake it up," Mari said. "Because he's not bluffing. If we don't go to him, he will unleash it."

Rose nodded, her face set in serious lines. Concern radiated from the rest of the council members. They shifted, clear signs of discomfort that I'd never seen them express before.

Hell, join the crowd.

I was pretty distressed by the idea myself.

"How do we defeat it?" I asked.

"You can't," Rose's said. "In all the times that it has risen, it has only ever been defeated once, by a Thunderbird. No one has seen a Thunderbird in centuries, and even if you found one, they cannot be commanded."

Shit. "So we have to stop him before he raises it. No matter what."

"Kerrin's vision of the future gave us some clues," Rose said. "The Great Serpent can only be raised if you possess the Gems of Katiana. There are three of them—the stone of darkness, stone of light, and stone of destiny—and once you have them, you can deploy them in any location to raise the serpent."

"He has the gems, doesn't he?" My mind raced. "Wait a second. He couldn't have them all. If he did, he'd want us to meet him now. He's giving himself time to collect them."

"Exactly." Rose nodded. "We know that the stone of darkness was held at the Temple of Indara in India. We checked into it, and there was a report of a great disturbance at the temple. An angel with black and white wings caused massive destruction."

"And got away with the gem," Mari said.

"Do we know where the last two are located?"

"No," Rose said. "There are rumors about the Middle East, maybe a castle, for the stone of light. But that's not a lot to go on. As for the stone of destiny, I don't know."

"It will have to be enough," I said. "We need to beat him to those gems, because turning myself over to him would make him more powerful than even the serpent."

"He must have a pretty good idea of where they are," Mari said. "He's given himself only three days to find the rest of them."

"Then we'll have to catch up to him." There was no other choice.

~

Moments later, Rose took us home. The council would be putting other slayers on the job, doing research and recon to try to find the stones, but I couldn't think about them right now. As far as I was concerned, it was just me and Mari on this one.

We appeared back in the underground cavern, silent and worried. Together, we raced up the stairs.

When we reached the main room, Mari turned to me. "I'm going to call the FireSouls. See if they know anything or can find anything. But I think Aethelred is also a possibility. He could see where the stones are, maybe."

The old seer lived just down the street, and she was right. There was every chance that he could maybe see a clue with his power. We needed to follow every lead we had.

"What can we give him?" I asked, knowing that Aethelred

preferred payment. Bribes, I liked to think of them. Mari was closest with him, so she'd know what he wanted.

"Normally I'd say he wanted Cornish pasties from Potions & Pastilles, but I don't want to head all the way down there to pick them up. So raid the liquor closet. See if you can find a bottle of that fancy old wine he likes. The stuff that the earl gave us as a gift."

I couldn't even remember the earl's name, but we'd saved him from a demon a couple years ago and he occasionally sent us fancy bottles of wine that we stashed away for bribing purposes.

"On it." I met her gaze, catching sight of the fear in her eyes. She had to be mentally reliving her time in Acius's captivity. After our childhood, we were both particularly sensitive about being locked up. I reached for her hand and squeezed. "Don't worry. We'll get him."

"We have to. Because I'll die before I go back to him."

"You won't have to. I'll make sure of it."

Together, we closed the secret door and put the table back in place. I raced out into the main part of the house, spotting Declan as he descended the stairs in clean clothes and with damp hair.

When he saw me, he frowned. "What happened? You look worried."

"Acius is back. Come on." As he followed me to the liquor cabinet, I explained what was going on and about how Acius wanted me.

"Shit," he said. "I've heard myths about the Great Serpent, but thought it was a fairy tale."

I snagged a bottle of wine out of the cupboard and looked at him over my shoulder. I could feel the wry twist to my mouth. "We're myths to a lot of people, so I'm not surprised the Great Serpent exists."

"Good point. I can ask a contact at the angel headquarters if they know anything about the location of the gems."

"Thanks." I held up the wine. "We can use this to see if Aethelred knows anything. And Mordaca is asking the FireSouls."

Please let someone know something.

Because otherwise, we were screwed.

3

Five minutes later, the three of us stood on the front stoop of Aethelred's house. I impatiently tapped my foot as we waited for the old seer to answer the door.

"He better be home," I muttered.

"He doesn't go to his country house until summer."

I didn't argue that Aethelred didn't have a country house *exactly*. It was more like a country tree. When the weather got warm, Aethelred moved into a tree out in the woods. True, it had furniture and plumbing, but it was still a tree. When he was in the city, he lived only a few doors down from us, which was convenient.

Finally, the blue door creaked open, and the old man peered out.

As usual, he was wearing one of his blue velour tracksuits, with his long white beard tucked into the trousers. He looked like Gandalf on his way to aerobics, but no one ever told him that. He was the most powerful seer in Magic's Bend, and you didn't want to be on his bad side.

"Hi, Aethelred," I said.

His blue eyes went immediately to the bottle of wine in my hand. "What do you want this time?"

"A vision." Mari stepped in without being invited. "And it's important, so no fussing."

He grumbled but didn't kick us out. He and Mari were pretty close, though they made a weird pair. Once a week, they took a walk on the beach for exercise, but he always had to bribe her with bacon sandwiches to get her to wake up that early.

I gestured for Declan to follow us in, then stepped inside Aethelred's dark, cluttered apartment.

He led us to an overfull living room that had knickknacks on every surface. The blinds were partially drawn, and dust motes glinted in the air. He took a seat in a worn old chair, and the three of us crowded onto the couch.

Even now, my heart was beating faster. It seemed like it'd picked up the pace as soon as I'd seen the projection of the Great Serpent and hadn't slowed down. Visions of the beast going all Godzilla on my town flashed through my mind.

Aethelred gestured for the bottle of wine, and I handed it over. We waited while he squinted at the label, then nodded and set it down. Finally, he looked at each of us in turn.

"Well, how's the world going to end this time?" he asked.

"How'd you know?" I said at the exact same time Mari said, "Not the whole world. Not yet."

"When you young whippersnappers come visiting with gifts, something bad is always about to happen. Trouble follows you around like a curse."

"I like to think we head out to meet trouble," Mari said.

Aethelred grumbled. "Six of one, half a dozen of another."

I gestured to Declan. "This is our friend Declan. He's going to help us."

"Angel, huh?" He squinted at Declan. "Fallen. Not evil." He looked at me. "Important to you."

I felt like my granddad had called me out in front of my crush, and my cheeks heated just slightly. Which was freaking annoying. I was too old for this crap, and I'd never had a granddad. Not one that I'd known, at least.

"That's beside the point," I said, and went on to explain about the Great Serpent and the three gems that would allow someone to awaken him and call him directly to Magic's Bend.

"And you want me to tell you the location of these gems." Aethelred frowned. "That'll be tough."

"Can you try?" Mari asked. "We just need to know about two of them."

Aethelred laughed, and the dust motes glittering around his head seemed to move faster, as if they were laughing, too. "Oh, well, that's all! Just see into the eternal ether and pluck out two very specific pieces of information."

"You *are* the best." Mari shrugged. "If anyone could do it, we thought it would be you. But if you can't..."

"I never said that." He sounded peeved, and I knew Mari was playing him like a violin and she was first chair. "Let me see what I can find."

We sat tense. Silent.

Aethelred worked, which was really just him sitting motionless in his chair while his magic flared. It took so long that I wanted to lean over and shake him. I wasn't particularly patient when it came to things like this.

At one point, Wally appeared next to me, sitting on the couch. His flame red eyes were pinned to Aethelred and his fur wafted wildly.

Old dude is going to tire himself out.

"Shhhh," I hissed at him.

Aethelred's eyes snapped open, and he glared at me. Then at Wally.

"You were not invited," Aethelred said to Wally.

Tell him that if he's nice to me, I won't hock up a hairball in a secret place for him to discover later.

I sighed. "I can't tell him that."

"Tell me what?" Aethelred demanded.

"Wally is sorry for appearing uninvited. He's just anxious to know what you can see about this matter."

Wally hissed, but Aethelred seemed satisfied.

He leaned back and put his hands on his knees. "Well, I was able to look into the past. Just a bit. At one point, the stone of light was protected by the Knights Templar."

"The Crusaders?" Declan asked.

Aethelred nodded. "The very same. They took it to one of their greatest castles in Syria. Krak des Chevaliers. It should still be there."

Perfect. Acius didn't expect us to have an ace like Aethelred up our sleeve. We might just beat him to the gem, and he'd never see it coming.

"And the other gem?" Mari asked.

"Somewhere near the North Sea. An island, maybe?"

I leaned forward, bracing my elbows on my knees. "Can you tell us anything more about either location? Any kind of hint?"

"The North Sea location is a mystery. You'll need to search the whole area." He frowned. "The castle though... I can see more about that."

Aethelred spelled out as much as he could, but it only got us closer, not all the way. He was able to describe the rough location of the castle in Syria, but there were multiple castles near the coast.

Ten minutes later, we left.

"I'm going to check in with the FireSouls again," Mari said as we climbed the stairs to our house.

I nodded and debated which target to hit up first. Where would Acius go?

There was no way to tell, so we'd have to divide and conquer. It was the only way.

"I know a guy in Syria," Declan said as we went into my kitchen.

Out of habit, I used the bell on the corner to order Chinese takeout. We'd need to fuel up fast, because I didn't think we'd get another chance.

While I waited for the magical charm to let the Jade Lotus know what I wanted, I looked at Declan. "Do you think he might know which castle to start at?"

"Better than we do. And he can hook us up with transportation. There are a few human settlements in the area. I can't be flying around looking for it without being seen."

I nodded. That was the last thing we needed.

The food appeared on the counter, having shot through the portal from the place down the street. I gathered up the three containers and brought them to the table. He joined me, and I pushed a container toward him, then took one for myself.

I opened it, pleased to see that they'd sent lo mein this time. Declan had Mongolian beef.

I eyed it. "Wally will want you to share."

He grinned. "I can spare some."

"Then how about a bite for me?"

I leaned over, and he fed me a bite of the savory goodness. I nipped the morsel from his chopsticks and chewed.

"Not bad for a first date." I shrugged. "I might not have gotten to change out of my fight wear, but the food's not bad."

"There's a bit more stress involved than I'd have liked." His tone was deadpan, and I grinned.

"Not a big fan of the possible destruction of Magic's Bend?"

"Can't say I am."

We turned our attention to our food, and ate quickly. Mari

returned a moment later, sitting heavily in her chair and dragging the white takeout container closer.

"The FireSouls can't sense anything from here. Not enough info and we're too far away," she said. "Del and Nix are off hunting an artifact that has so much decayed magic stored up inside it that it could destroy a village in Norway, so they're busy. But Cass can come to the North Sea with me to help me look."

"Perfect." I set down my chopsticks. "Declan has a friend in Syria who can hook us up with some transport and maybe a more exact location for the castle."

Mari nodded. "Good. At least we have a plan."

"Now all we've got to do is save Magic's Bend."

Half an hour later, Declan and I arrived in a tiny village in Syria. We'd used a transport charm to appear at the entrance to a quiet little bar. It was night there, late enough that the place was almost empty.

Good.

All the better for sneaking around.

Declan led the way into the small, low-ceilinged bar. It wasn't a fancy place, but it was inviting. There were only a few patrons, both of them human, but they seemed to be having a nice chat instead of drowning their sorrows.

Declan approached the small wooden bar, which was unmanned. He leaned over it and called in a soft voice, "Abbad?"

A few seconds later, a dark-haired man appeared from a door at the back. A wide grin split across his face, revealing the whitest teeth I'd ever seen. I could feel the slightest pulse of magic coming from him. It felt like a hot summer sun on my skin. His patrons might not be supernaturals, but he was.

"Declan!" He sounded genuinely pleased to see the fallen angel. "What brings you here? And who is your lovely friend?"

Declan lowered his voice. "This is Aerdeca, and we're here with a bit of a problem."

Abbad's eyes sharpened immediately. "I see." He gestured for us to follow him. "Come to the back, then."

He led us to a tiny room in the back and grabbed a few bottles of cold beer. I took mine with a nod of thanks, then sat at the only table in the room. It was a tiny thing, only big enough to hold four.

Abbad sat heavily and rested his elbows on his knees. "I should have known you weren't just here for a visit."

"Sorry, friend. Haven't had the time."

He shook his head. "Always saving the world."

"Trying to." A wry smile pulled at Declan's lips.

Determined to cut right to the chase and get this party started, I leaned forward. "We're looking for an ancient Templar castle that could hold a gem capable of raising the Great Serpent. We think it's one of the castles in this area."

Abbad's brows rose. "Ah, yes." He nodded slowly. "There is only one such place. Not easy to get to. And you certainly won't want to reach it, once you get close."

"Repelling charms?" Declan asked.

"Bad ones. The castle was inhabited by supernaturals when it was a Templar stronghold. It was the only one that held magical beings in the area, so I think it is the most likely candidate to contain your gem."

"It's uninhabited now?" I asked. "Not a tourist attraction or anything?"

He shook his head. "When the Templars died out, it stayed abandoned. Their magic imbues the place, keeping away humans and supernaturals alike. Some say it is haunted."

"With our luck lately, I'm sure it is," I said. "How far away is it?"

"An hour by motorbike, high in the hills away from any settlements."

"Can we transport there?" Declan asked.

Abbad shook his head. "No. The protections will prevent it. You're about as close as you can get, now. But I can loan you the motorbikes."

"Can we buy them?" Declan asked. "I doubt we'll have a chance to return them."

Abbad sighed, but nodded. "That is fine. The protections that guard the place may destroy the bikes anyway."

"What do you know about them?" Declan asked.

"Besides the feeling that pushes you back, I've heard rumor of explosions. Avoid the places that rumble from within the earth."

Yeah, I'd have done that anyway. I wanted no part of a rumbling earth.

It didn't take long for Abbad to get us set up with two rusty old motorbikes. They were more like dirt bikes than actual motorcycles, and they looked like they'd seen better days.

Abbad pointed into the distance, to where the moonlight beamed on rolling hills. "Head toward the moon. The road will stop, but keep going in that direction. You will know you are close when you want to turn back. Keep going, and you will see the stronghold on the top of the hill."

"Thank you, old friend." Declan clapped Abbad on the back, and he took us to the rear of the bar where a collection of ramshackle motorbikes were parked.

We paid for two, which rumbled like angsty old cars, and we set off down the road. It took a little while to get the hang of it—I wasn't used to motorbikes on dirt roads—but with the wind whipping through my hair and the moon high above, it was pretty damned cool. If I ignored the reason I was out there.

Soon, the road ended, and we had to cut across scrubby ground. Tiny mounds of earth and clumps of grass made for a bumpy ride, but it was better than walking.

We'd ascended two hills by the time the air started to prickle with discomfort.

Turn back.

The desire screamed through me. It felt like I had something I needed to do back home. Danger lurked all around.

"Do you feel that?" I shouted.

"Yeah. It's strong."

I revved my motorbike so I rode alongside Declan. A frown slashed across his face, and his brow wrinkled. The air felt like hundreds of tiny bugs were biting me, but I couldn't see them.

Magic.

I gritted my teeth and kept my head down, making sure to keep my bike pointed toward the moon. Had Acius already traveled this way?

I hoped not.

When I spotted the castle on a hill in the distance, grim satisfaction seethed through me. The moonlight gleamed off of the enormous white structure. The daylight must have bleached the stones, because it looked ivory under the pale light. The whole thing was enormous—maybe the biggest castle I'd ever seen, complete with huge walls and a roof that looked as good as new.

"It doesn't look abandoned," Declan said.

I could feel the ghostly energy in the air. Cold and biting, it reminded me of being with the evil ghost girl back in the Chateau d'If, the prison in France.

"I don't think it's people who live there," I said, pitching my voice over the roar of the motors.

As we ascended the last hill, approaching the castle from below, the ground beneath us began to vibrate.

"Shit, you feel that?" I asked.

"Yeah. Stronger from the left."

I could just barely sense that, so I veered my bike right. Not a moment too soon. A patch of land to the left exploded, sending dirt and debris flying high. The air vibrated with the force, slamming into me and nearly bowling me over.

They were like magical land mines. Ancient ones, from the feel of the magic. It felt like old dust under my fingertips, grainy and horrible. It smelled of age—that dry, abandoned scent of a house too long uninhabited.

"There's a trigger if we get too close," I shouted, pushing out with my magic to try to sense if there were any more bombs nearby. I was fairly good at sensing magic, and if I focused, I could just barely feel the areas that vibrated with more of it.

I tried to avoid them, swerving left and right, but they exploded all the same. Every time, a blast of energy slammed into my skin, dirt and rocks pelting me. If I hit one directly, I'd be screwed. My heart thundered in my ears, competing with the sound of the howling wind.

As I navigated the tricky terrain, I prayed that whoever had set these out here was long dead and not looking out of the castle, watching our approach. Could ghosts fight us? Phantoms could, but ghosts were often a different matter.

We were only halfway up the hill when the magical signature of the bombs increased exponentially. It was the only warning I had. My bike rolled right over the top of one, and the blast shot me high into the air.

My stomach surged as I disconnected from the bike and caught sight of a flash of ground beneath me.

I had only one thought blaring in my mind. *If I fall wrong, I'll break my neck.*

4

Terror froze my muscles as I tumbled through the air. I tried to twist to land in a way that wouldn't kill me, but it was nearly impossible to control my motions in the air.

Out of the corner of my eye, I spotted a flash of movement. At the last possible second, Declan drove his motorbike right under me and managed to catch me with one arm.

My legs dragged the ground and the bike nearly tipped over, but he was able to right it. I scrambled onto the bike behind him, clinging to his waist.

"Holy fates, that was close." My chest was so tight I almost couldn't breathe. "Thanks."

"Anytime." He slowed the bike. "It's nearly impossible to feel exactly where they are here."

Wally appeared in front of us, his black fur wafting wildly on the wind. He turned back, his flame-red eyes flickering. *Follow me.*

I pointed over Declan's shoulder. "Follow Wally."

The little cat raced in a zigzag, his magic somehow sensing where the bombs were placed. I could still feel the vibrations, but they stayed fairly steady and faint. No more wild pulses when we went somewhere we shouldn't.

Sweat chilled on my skin as we approached the castle walls. They soared overhead, smooth white stone that reflected the moonlight. I saw no one on the castle walls—neither ghost nor person.

Despite the magic that swelled from the structure, it appeared totally empty. It had the dead feeling of a place long abandoned. Our motorbike engines didn't rouse even a bit of suspicion, from what I could see.

Wally approached the castle wall, then stopped, his back arched and his smoky fur poofed out to twice its normal size.

"He doesn't like it," Declan said.

Strong magic. Wally's voice drifted back to me. *Avoid the walls. We need a gate.*

"Find a gate," I translated for Declan. "There's something about the walls that's deadly."

Declan slowed the bike as we approached, finding a bit of flat ground that surrounded the walls. Dark magic pulsed from them, some kind of charm that made me want to retch and die simultaneously.

"Yeah, I agree with Wally." I shuddered, wrapping my arms tighter around Declan.

As he drove around the perimeter of the castle, I kept my gaze trained on the wall above. Nothing, so far. But with such strong repellent magic, I doubted this would be easy.

Finally, we found a massive wooden gate. Wally approached it slowly, sniffing at the wood. I could already feel that it wasn't as heavily guarded as the walls. It made sense. Good guys and bad guys alike had to get through the gate, whereas only bad guys would go over the wall. I had a feeling that whatever protected the massive white walls was enough to kill even the good guys who had permission to be there.

Declan killed the motorbike engine. I climbed off, and he followed.

He stepped back and tilted his neck to inspect the gate. “Doesn’t look like it’s been opened in centuries.”

He was right. There were streaks of rust where the bolts were bleeding onto the old wood. We paced the perimeter of the gate, looking for a way to raise it. There was nothing visible from out here, which was no surprise.

“Should we try flying over?” I asked. We were far enough away from settlements, and with those repelling charms, there was no one close enough to witness him defying gravity.

“I’ll test it.” His wings unfurled from his back, black and glorious. He launched himself into the air, flying gracefully to the top of the wall.

He’d just begun to cross over when dozens of arrows launched from the walls, heading straight for him.

“Declan!” I shouted, my heart jumping into my throat.

He jerked as one grazed his arm, then darted backward, away from the arrows. They flew in a mass, a wall of deadly wooden spikes. As soon he was away from the wall, they ceased flying.

He landed next to me, gripping his wounded arm.

I hurried toward him. “Are you okay?”

I pried his hand away to see a deep slice where the arrow had cut through him.

“Fine.” His voice was rough as his healing light shined. He used the power to repair his wound, and the skin knitted itself back together. “There were no guards on the wall, as expected. I triggered an ancient defense spell.”

“Let’s take the gate.” I inspected the old wood, feeling guilty about what I was going to suggest. “Can you light it up with a bit of holy fire? Since the rest of the structure is stone, it should only burn away the gate.”

"I can try." He approached the gate and raised his hand. Flickering flames danced in his palms. He hurled a blast right at the gate, then another.

I held my breath as the wood ignited. It burned away quickly, and even the metal studs melted into a puddle on the ground where the ashes of the gate piled up.

"I doubt regular flame could have done that," I said.

"Probably not. It was protected as well." He caught my eye. "But the good news is that Acius probably hasn't been here yet."

"Hopefully." I stepped on the pile of ash that littered the ground. As soon as I began to cross the threshold, magic sparked on the air. Hot and thick, it clogged my lungs and burned my skin.

"Come on!" Declan shouted. He clearly felt it, too.

Wally hissed loudly.

Intense fear flashed through me, a warning that propelled me forward. I lunged through the gate, instinct forcing me to look up.

A massive blob of black, boiling oil poured down, splashing on the ground behind me. A few small drops hit the back of my thighs, burning right through my clothes and making tears spring to my eyes.

I lunged away from the oil, panting hard.

I spun to face the gate, making sure that nothing else was coming and that Wally and Declan were okay.

The oil was a massive puddle beneath the gate, dripping down the hill. Declan and Wally stood near me, both wide-eyed.

"We triggered another ancient spell." What else was going to come at us?

"Are you—"

The ground beneath our feet shook, cutting off Declan's words. We stood on a strip of land that looked a bit like an empty moat surrounding the castle. The wall that we'd just walked through had only been the *first* set of walls. There was a ring of barren land between it and the main castle wall, which rose up in front of us, not quite as high as the other.

Two defensive barriers, separated by no man's land.

The ground shook harder, and I stumbled toward Declan, grabbing onto his shoulder. My heart raced, thundering in my ears.

Something is coming! Wally's voice sounded from near my ankles. *From down below.*

As soon as he'd said the words, massive spikes began to jut up from the ground beneath our feet. They were four feet tall and sharp as thorns. Dozens popped up randomly. Any second now, they'd pierce us from below.

Declan grabbed me around the waist and launched himself into the air.

"Get out of here!" I shouted down at Wally.

He disappeared in a flash.

Declan flew us toward the second wall. Magic pricked against my skin, sharp and painful.

A warning.

I drew my shield from the ether, just in time. Declan flew over the second wall, into the main castle compound, and the arrows started flying.

I tucked my legs in against Declan and held the shield facing down, toward the arrows that flew toward us. They pinged off the metal shield, hitting with such force that my arm hurt.

As Declan had said, there were no people or ghosts shooting the arrows. We'd triggered some kind of spell, and they'd started flying.

As soon as we'd crossed over the thick wall, Declan dropped down into the main castle courtyard. We landed with a thud, and Declan tilted to the left.

I scrambled out of his arms.

Shit, was he injured?

Blood seeped from a wound where an arrow had pierced his calf. My stomach lurched.

"What can I do?" I knelt by the wound.

"Nothing." His voice was rough with pain as he bent down and broke the quills off the arrow. Then he yanked it through, wincing only slightly.

My stomach pitched, and I turned from him to inspect our surroundings, keeping a lookout while he healed himself. We stood in a large open area surrounded by huge stone buildings. It was empty, but ghostly energy pulsed on the air.

I shivered and rubbed my arms, then stood, making sure to keep the castle wall to my back. I didn't know what else this place would throw at us, but I didn't want it coming from behind.

"Man, this place is haunted," I murmured.

"Even I feel it." Declan's magic faded as he finished healing himself.

I called upon my new power to see ghosts. Sometimes they showed themselves to everyone. Sometimes they hid. My new gift, which I'd just created a week ago to try to find Acius, allowed me to see them even when they concealed themselves.

The first thing I spotted was the flags waving at the tops of the building. They glowed with a faint light. Very ghosty. It was impossible to make out the emblem on the fabric that whipped in the wind, but I had a feeling it would be the red cross of the Knights Templar.

I frowned. "I can see the ghostly shadow of their flag, but that's weird. An inanimate object isn't a ghost."

"Perhaps it's a ghost of the past."

"Could be." I didn't fully understand the new gift I'd created. I turned my attention to the area around us. Slowly, figures began to coalesce. The courtyard was full of warriors, many of them mounted. A few women moved here and there, bringing things to the men.

I frowned. Even in death, the women were waiting on the men.

Sucked.

I'd rather ride into battle than bring a dude his weapon any day.

One by one, the figures turned to look at me. They tilted their heads, blinking with confusion.

Shit!

I called upon my ghost magic, drawing it back into my body so the images of the ghosts faded away. Did this mean they couldn't see me? Or was I an ostrich sticking my head in the sand?

"What's going on?" Declan asked. "Your magic is going wild."

My skills at suppressing my magical signature while I used it still sucked, it seemed.

"There are a *lot* of ghosts here. Warrior ghosts with weapons and horses, servant ghosts. I think they could see me when I could see them." I waited for them to attack. To do something. Every hair on my body stood up, and my breathing turned shallow. "I don't know if they can see us now."

"I can't see them." Declan drew a shield, and I raised mine in front of me.

I hated not being able to see them, but this seemed like maybe the safest way to avoid them and all their weapons. And magic. This had been a supernatural Templar headquarters, so these people could easily be packing some pretty fierce magical firepower.

After a few moments, when nothing happened, my shoulders relaxed. "Let's head toward the interior."

Declan nodded.

We set off across the courtyard.

"Are we walking through ghosts right now?" Declan asked.

"Probably."

Near the main entrance of the biggest building, I caught another flash of blue movement. More ghosts.

Their figures weren't very clear, but they flickered in and out. All were looking at us.

I blinked, trying to force them away.

But they didn't go. They were determined to make themselves known, and I couldn't control it.

"Hurry," I said. "We need to get out of the courtyard. I think they can see us."

"Our clothes are too strange. We stand out."

"They'll know we're intruders."

Together, we walked as fast as we could through the main castle door.

The enormous entry room was dark, with just a bit of moonlight flickering through the windows. I grabbed Declan's hand and pulled him left, running toward a narrow corridor and then a nook in the wall. We tucked ourselves back into it.

Slowly, I called upon my magic, letting the ghosts in the space become visible.

A few servants passed by through the hall, and I could hear the sound of a party in the distance. It had been silent before. I was sure of it.

If Acius had come through here already, surely they would have noticed?

"Do you hear that?" I asked.

"Hear what?"

"There's a party going on, I think."

"I can't hear anything. Or see any ghosts."

"I'll be our eyes and ears, then. Come on. Let's keep to the shadows and go farther in. Maybe we can find out where they keep the valuables."

Together, we snuck through the corridors, headed toward the banquet. I didn't want to go all the way in, but I did want to get a feeling for how many people were there.

We reached the massive main hall and peeked through the door, catching sight of a huge gathering. Hundreds of ghosts sat at long tables, eating and drinking and making merry. Well, mostly the men were making merry. Once again, the women were hauling around heavy things and serving them. There were a few male servants, too, of course, but it was primarily women.

I ducked back into the safety of the empty hall and looked at Declan. "Yep, it's a big party." I grabbed Declan's hand. "Come on. Let's find the kitchens. Maybe we can find someone to ask about where they keep the valuables."

"You think they'll just tell us?"

"Not everyone is happy here. I'm sure we can find someone who is annoyed with the status quo and wouldn't mind letting the cat out of the bag."

I resent that.

I looked down to see Wally, who'd just appeared. "Resent what?"

The bit about the cat and the bag.

"It's a figure of speech."

He shrugged his shoulder. *Still don't like it.*

Normally, I'd joke with him. Now wasn't the time. We needed info, and if I couldn't sweet talk someone into telling me what I needed to know, I could charm them.

We followed the smell of cooking meat to a space that was a combo indoor/outdoor kitchen. Dozens of women and some men worked back there, most of them looking pretty miserable.

I scanned the space, finally spotting a serving girl who scowled as she loaded up a tray.

I pointed to her. "There's a serving girl over there. Let's intercept her."

He nodded and we moved quickly, keeping to the edge of the large cooking area as we aimed to meet up with her at the entrance to another hall.

She got there before us, and I hurried, entering the dimly lit stone corridor after her.

"Hey!" I called in a low voice.

She stiffened and tilted her head, as if she could almost hear me but wasn't sure.

"Hey, you!" Did they even *say* "hey" back in the days of the Crusaders? That was almost a thousand years ago. I should be able to understand her since I had been able to understand the evil prison ghost last week.

There'd be a huge cultural barrier though. This woman was from eleventh-century Syria. In fairness, she could be a pilgrim from Europe. Maybe I was being really rude to her by shouting *hey*?

"Excuse me! Pardon!"

Finally, she stopped and turned. She blinked at us, clearly confused by our clothes, then spoke, the words a garbled language in another tongue.

Shit.

I focused on my magic, trying to increase my connection with her. Because that's what this magic was, right? It was the ability to make connections with the dead. Why shouldn't that transcend language? Surely, if I tried hard enough, I'd be able to understand her intentions like I had last time.

I sucked in a deep breath and focused on my new magic. My connection with the ghost was almost a physical thing. I imagined it as a thread that connected us, and I fed my magic into it, trying to strengthen it.

I approached. "Hello."

"Is person there?" She squinted at me. She looked young, but tired. "You are ghostly."

I grinned as excitement shot through me. The language wasn't perfect—I could still hear the foreign words—but I could understand her intentions.

"I'm not a ghost."

She tilted her head again. "You look like a ghost."

Shit. I couldn't tell her *she* was a ghost. Maybe she knew? But I didn't want to tell her she was a specter, acting out her life long after death.

Definitely ignore those *details.*

I stopped about five feet in front of her, Declan at my side. I pointed to him. "Can you see him?"

She looked to my left, her frown increasing. "See who?"

Okay, that was news. The protections around the castle could hurt him, but the ghosts couldn't see him. Made sense, since the protections had been hanging around for thousands of years and had originally been put in place to stop living invaders of any species or magical origin.

"Don't worry about it." I considered using my coolest, most commanding voice. It worked on most people. But people commanded her all day long, and she probably had no choice but to obey. I didn't want to add to it. "We are looking for something. Will you help us?"

She inspected my clothing, looking up and down. "You are dressed like a man, but you are a woman. Are you a heathen?"

I frowned. Yeah, I probably was a heathen. Especially in her eyes. "I'm from the future."

Her brows rose. "The future?"

She had a bit of magic—I could feel a signature that reminded me of soft cotton beneath my fingertips—so she wasn't unfamiliar with magic. It wouldn't be so crazy to her.

I nodded. "Yes, the future. It has many interesting things. Like pants. And women's rights."

She tilted her head. "Women's...rights?"

I sighed, wanting to explain more, but there was no time. She was already dead, anyway. Perhaps I could come back and try to get a ghostly women's revolution going. *After* we'd stopped Acius.

"We are looking for the place where you might keep the treasures of the Crusades. The things that you protect."

Suspicion flashed on her face. "Why?"

"In the future, an evil fallen angel is trying to destroy my town with one of those objects. I need to get to it before he does."

She scoffed. "That is ridiculous."

"As ridiculous as you being able to see a ghost from the future?"

She frowned, nodding her head to concede that it was a valid point. "I could get in trouble."

We didn't have time for this.

Quickly, I sliced my finger with my sharp thumbnail. Pain, then blood. Finally, magic.

I swiped my finger over her forehead. "Please help us."

I imbued the words with my suggestive magic and she twitched. Her features relaxed, then concern darkened her eyes. "The evil angel will destroy your town?"

"Yes. Thousands of people will die. And remember, we're from the future. I'm not technically here right now. We're crossing time to speak. So, when I take the gem, it won't be removed from your time, just mine."

She sighed, then looked around, clearly concerned that someone could hear. "All right. There is a cavern deep beneath the castle. It is guarded by the holy one Baphomet. It is very dangerous, but it is where we protect the treasures collected on the Crusades. It is the reason that this castle was built here."

"Thank you. How do we get there?"

"You must go through the great hall, where the dining is happening. Then through the wide passage and to the door at the bottom. If you can get past the Wise Mistress, you will be under the castle. From there, I do not know. It is dangerous, but you will find what you seek."

"Thank you."

She inclined her head, then gestured forward. "Come with me, I will lead you through the hall. It is difficult to see your form, so if I stand between you and the crowd, they may not see you."

"I appreciate that." I looked at Declan. "Ready?"

"She's leading us to the treasure?"

I nodded, realizing that he hadn't been able to hear her side of the conversation—just me saying thank you a lot.

"Then I'm ready," he said. "Let's go."

The serving girl turned and led us through the hall. I could hear the sound of revelry as we neared it. Shouts and songs and chatter.

We entered behind the serving girl, and as she'd promised, she stuck to the side wall. I kept my gaze glued to the warriors who sat at the tables, eating and drinking. Though they weren't wearing armor, they all had a weapon at hand.

Could they hurt us? Or would their blades go right through?

I hoped it was the latter.

A few of them turned to look as we passed, but their frowns didn't become anything more. They didn't get up or charge us. By the time we reached the far end of the Great Hall, my heart was thundering in my ears.

"This is where I leave you," she said.

"Thank you." I swiped my bloodied finger over her forehead

once more, imbuing my voice with my magic. “Forget of me, I will of thee.”

Her eyes fogged, and she drifted away, taking her platter to the high table where the leader sat.

Declan and I darted into the wide back passageway. Torches flickered on the wall, thin spires of black smoke twisting upward toward blackened spots on the ceiling. The stone was pale and smooth, so different than other castles that I’d been inside.

“She couldn’t see me at all, then?” Declan asked.

“No. I don’t think any of the ghosts can.” But I had no idea if that was to our advantage, or not.

We made it to the end of the hall, which turned right. As soon as we’d entered, I caught sight of a group of warriors. Four of them, all looking sweaty and like they’d been out fighting. They wore the white fabric with the red cross that was the uniform of the Templars, but the fabric was marred by dust. Underneath the tunic they wore chain-mail armor.

Their eyes zeroed in on me immediately.

Shit.

5

"INTRUDER!" A KNIGHT POINTED AT ME, AND A SCOWL CREASED HIS face behind his beard.

All four drew their swords.

I tried to disassociate from my magic so we could no longer see each other, but one of them spoke before I could. "It's a whore in the garb of a man!"

"Um, what?" I glared at him. I was *so* not here for this.

Sure, maybe in their culture, women did not wear pants. But it wasn't like the women got to *choose.* It was dudes like this who enforced that patriarchal bullshit.

The exhaustion on the serving girl's face flashed in my mind's eye. She didn't have any choice in life except to serve these guys beer and hunks of meat.

I strode toward them, drawing my mace from the ether. "First, no man dresses as well as I do. Second, even if I *was* a whore, whatever. And it's not like it's any of your business."

Their jaws dropped, then they glared.

"We should stone her," said one with a massive mustache.

I laughed. "*Stone* me?"

Did the Knights Templar even *do* that? Or were these guys just assholes all on their own?

Did it matter?

"I'll teach her a lesson," said another.

"Okay, that offends me more than the possible stoning." I frowned. "Though maybe it should be a tie?"

"Stoning?" Declan asked from beside me. "What the hell is going on?"

"Just a little lesson, is all." I focused on the magical signatures that filled the air. The men had magic, but not a lot of it. I was getting weak hits of their signatures—the scent of cloves, the sound of iron being struck. One guy had a faint blue aura.

"Who is she talking to?" asked the tallest man. He stood closest to me, so I assumed he was the leader.

"I would like to pass." I gestured to the hallway behind them. "Will you let me?"

I already knew the answer.

"Grab her," said the tall man. "She's an intruder. We'll take her to the dungeons."

I frowned at him. "I was worried you'd say that. And I'm certain you'll regret it."

He scoffed. "I don't regret anything."

I grinned and began to swing my mace.

One of the men laughed. "She wields a weapon!"

Wally appeared next to me. *I'm really looking forward to this.*

I looked down at him. "You would, you bloodthirsty beast."

"She has a hellcat!" One of the men stumbled back.

"I'm afraid you're going to have to stay out of this one, Wally. These guys need to be taught a lesson."

I love teaching lessons.

"By a woman."

Wally's whiskers dropped, but he nodded. *I understand. I'll save How to Get Murdered 101 for later. Surely someone will need a tutorial.*

I laughed, then charged the men, who raised their swords, looking confused. I was sure there were female warriors from this time period, but these guys had clearly never run into one.

The leader's blade shot through with fire, which would probably send hot sparks toward me if I fought him with my own sword.

I was close enough to the man with the fire blade that I was able to smash the mace into his side before he could swing his sword. It slammed into his chain mail, and he went flying into the wall. He clashed against it, metal clanging, then slumped to the ground. The flame on his sword died down.

Two of the men charged, their blades raised. I ducked one sword, then kicked the guy in the stomach as I swung my mace at the other. The metal ball crashed against his shoulder, and he howled, then went down with a clang. I spun around to hit the first attacker, but he was too fast.

Magically fast, and skilled with the blade.

Unfortunately for him, I was also extra fast. Though his sword was headed right toward my neck, it was easy to duck again. I felt the whoosh of steel fly past my hair, then I kicked him in the stomach once more. It was repetitive, but why fix what wasn't broken?

Ooh, get him again! Wally cheered from the sidelines.

Declan stood next to him, arms crossed and brow furrowed. He could only see my side of the battle, and he clearly didn't enjoy being left out. He waited anyway, watching as I kicked ass. He trusted me to be able to handle myself. Good.

Anyway, I could probably use my ghost suit if I needed the advantage. But I wanted these bastards to see what was coming at them.

Before the knight could recover his swing, I heaved my mace

at his shoulder. Normally, I'd go for the head, but killing wasn't my purpose here.

The fourth guy charged, his face twisted in anger and a little bit of fear. I liked that last bit.

"Let's make it a little more even." I stashed my mace in the ether and drew my blade.

We'd need to make this quick. The men on the ground were groaning and trying to rise again, and I didn't have time to kick their asses a second time. Or have them go alert the rest of the castle.

The approaching warrior had an evil twist to his lips as he swung the blade at my middle.

"Going for the easy shot?" I darted out of the way.

He growled and tried again, but I whirled around faster than he could move and slammed my blade into his side. The steel didn't penetrate his armor, but it knocked the wind from him. While he was gasping, I smashed the hilt of my blade against his skull.

He dropped to the ground, unconscious.

The three other men cringed back, too wounded to put up a good fight. None of them would die, but they'd think twice before assuming a woman was weaker than them.

"Try to do better, dudes," I said as I sliced my finger with my thumbnail. Blood welled. I darted from man to man, moving as quickly as I could. I swiped my finger across the forehead of each man and used my suggestive magic. "Forget of me, I will of these. Don't be a dick to women. And go to sleep for four hours."

I was pretty sure they didn't use the term *be a dick*, but I was sure they got the drift.

Each man passed out, head slumping weakly to the side.

"Coast is clear?" Declan asked.

I looked up at him and grinned. "Sure is. Let me take care of these jerks."

Normally Declan would help with body disposal, but he couldn't actually see them, so it was all on me. I dragged them to an alcove and shoved them against the wall, out of sight. When I returned to Declan, he frowned at me.

"Can't say I'm a fan of watching you fight and not being able to help."

I shrugged. "I had it under control."

"I know. Doesn't mean I don't want to help."

I smiled and squeezed his arm. Considering how many times he'd saved my life in the past few weeks, I definitely appreciated his desire to help.

We continued down the hall. With the fight over, Wally had decided to head elsewhere, but he'd be back.

The hall curved gently downward, past a chapel built into the main part of the castle. The domed space was quiet as we passed it by. About twenty yards down the hall, magic began to fill the air.

"You feel that?" I whispered.

"For the first time, yeah. Can you see anything?"

"No." The hall was empty.

Ten yards later, we reached a bend in the wide stone hall. The magic was strongest there, pulsing with a fierce energy that both repelled and terrified. There was someone near. Someone massively powerful.

Declan clearly felt it, too, because his brow was creased with concern and his steps totally silent. I held out my hand to indicate that he should stop, then paused at the corner of the wall and peered around.

A woman stood in front of a massive wooden door. She wore a glorious green dress and looked to be almost in a trance. Her auburn hair tumbled over her shoulders, and magic flickered around her palms. Normally, I'd consider that to be a weapon that was about to be hurled at my face.

Right then, however, it seemed to be more like a permanent state of being for her. Like she had so much magic it wanted to spill out of her at all times.

Seriously? With a woman this tough, it was surprising those warriors from earlier didn't have more respect for women fighters.

But then, there were exceptions for everything. Especially in the magical world. They probably attributed her strength to her magic and not her femininity.

Morons. It was both.

I ducked back behind the edge of the wall and stood up on my tiptoes. Declan leaned down so I could whisper in his ear. "I think she's a guard. That must be the entrance to the underground cavern full of the Templars' treasures."

"She's too powerful to fight without causing some serious damage to the building."

He was right. The overflow of magic from our battle would definitely draw attention to us.

"We need to convince her to let us through." I wracked my mind. "But there's no way my suggestion magic will work on her. I wouldn't even be able to get close enough to try."

I bit my lip, searching for an alternative. "Hang on a sec..."

"What's your idea?"

I grinned up at Declan. "This might not work, and she might not be into it. But she's part of this Knights Templar guild. They're very religious, which probably means she's pretty into angels."

"And I'm an angel..."

"But she can't see you."

"Yet?" He gave me a look. "You sound like you're going to say 'yet.'"

"That's what I'm not sure will work. But I want to try." I held up my hand, moving my fingers as I imagined manipulating my new ghost magic.

There were boundaries on it, of course. But I didn't *know* those boundaries. When I made new magic, I just did it with my imagination and knowledge of the magical world. I had an idea of what ghost whisperers could do.

But could I expand that?

"I'm going to try to make you visible to her," I said. "I'll bring you to the same spirit plane that we walk upon. Then, once she can see you, sweet talk our way through that gate."

"If she's been appointed by a religious order to guard their most valuable treasures, I don't think she's going to fall for sweet talking," he said.

I leaned to the side to look at the woman again. "Yeah, she does look pretty serious." I pulled back and looked at him. "Well, whatever you decide to try, I'm sure you'll figure it out. Ready?" I held up my hand and wiggled my fingers.

He nodded. "More than."

Yeah, he clearly didn't like hanging out in the background and letting me do all the fighting.

I touched his shoulder. "Think ghosty thoughts."

"What the hell is a ghosty thought?"

"I don't know. Imagine yourself as transparent. Floaty. Ephemeral." I pursed my lips. "It'd probably help if you tried to connect with my magic. I know that sounds a bit floofy, but you get what I'm saying."

"Basically. Let's do this."

I nodded and began to feed my magic into him. The ghost power was becoming easier to call upon, and it rose to the surface within me, surging bright. I tried to force it into Declan, imagining it binding with his essence to make him part of the spectral world.

Nothing happened.

Hmm.

I tried connecting my magic to his. It was a weird process, but I felt my way through it. When I touched him like this and tried to feed my magic into his body—his soul, even—a connection formed between us. I could feel him—who he was.

Good. Declan was fundamentally good, despite the fact that he'd fallen from heaven.

"I feel that," he murmured.

"Good. Now think ghosty." I kept pushing my magic toward him, trying to join our magical signatures in a way that would allow him to communicate with the powerful woman in the hall.

After a moment, something snapped in the air. A bit of magic that felt like a cold whoosh past my face.

"I feel it," Declan said. "It's definitely working."

"Take a peek at the mage. See if you can see her now."

He looked around the edge of the wall. "It worked."

"Perfect. I'm going to try to stop it now." I drew back on the ghost magic. It was reluctant to leave Declan, but finally, I felt it suck back into my body.

"I no longer see her now."

"What about now?" I said, pushing my magic into him and feeling like an eye doctor asking if A or B was clearer.

"I see her."

I tugged him back toward me. Confidence surged through me. I was getting good with this new magic. Controlling it. Manipulating it.

"Aeri." Declan's gaze met mine, and his voice was low. "Your magical signature has decreased."

My brows shot up. "Really?"

"Really. It must be because you're controlling this new magic. Manipulating it and making it your own."

Oh wow. He had a point. I was doing totally new things with

this gift—proving that I was the master of it. Not the other way around.

I *was* in control.

The fear that had hovered at the edges of my consciousness faded a bit.

Was that the key? Focus on controlling the magic, not the signature? Go back to the source?

It helped me control my fear, so yeah, it made sense.

I pressed a quick, hard kiss to his lips, then drew back. "You're pretty smart, you know that?"

He grinned. "And you're pretty powerful. Keep working on it."

"Oh, I will. And in the meantime, we've got to get this gem." I leaned closer. "Here's our plan... It only takes me a couple seconds to make you visible to her. Let's sneak up on her first—I'll be invisible with my ghost suit and you'll just be normal—then I'll feed my magic into you and bam! You'll appear in front of her like an all-powerful angel." I frowned. "She won't be able to tell you're fallen, right?"

"Probably not. She won't know what to look for, and the wings are usually enough to fool anyone." Declan flared his wings wide, then frowned. "I should be wearing heavenly robes, though."

"How's she to know what real angels wear? You guys probably don't come down to talk to these people often, right?"

"No, definitely not. Crusaders could be a bit...intense."

"Well, then." I gestured to his clothes. "This is Angel Chic, and she has no way to know any differently. Own it."

He gave me a cocky grin. "Not a problem."

"That's the spirit. I'm going to flip up my invisibility hood now. It'll be all you."

"Got it."

I grabbed his shirt and tugged slightly. "I'll hang on to you so you know where I am. In case a fight breaks out."

He nodded.

The last thing either of us wanted was to mistakenly behead the other one. Talk about a shitty start to a relationship. Sorta Romeo and Juliet, but bloodier and a bit more ridiculous.

I flipped up my hood. "Let's go. T-minus ten seconds until you're ghosty."

Declan strode out of the hall and around the corner, heading toward the woman who stood at the end. I made sure to keep my footsteps silent as I stuck by him.

Tension tightened my muscles, but within seconds, it was clear she couldn't see either of us.

Her magic rolled over me with an intensity that made a shiver race down my spine. Damn, she was trouble. Definitely a lot of offensive magic—I could hear the clang of swords and feel a punch to the gut as I neared her.

We stopped ten feet in front of her. She tilted her head and sniffed the air, clearly trying to figure out what had changed. She couldn't see either of us—thank fates my invisibility worked on her—but she could sense that something had changed.

I fed my magic into Declan, imagining him joining the spectral plane and becoming visible to the ghostly mage.

She gasped, and I assumed he'd appeared. He looked normal to me no matter what, since I wasn't a ghost.

Declan's magic surged through the air as his wings flared from his back. I blew out a surprised breath.

Wow.

Normally he kept it mostly contained. He wasn't one to be flashy with his power under most circumstances, but this called for an impressive display.

Declan cleared his throat slightly, then boomed, "Most

valued servant, you have protected the treasures of the heavens. The angels are most grateful."

"The angels?" Her eyes roved over his wings.

He gave his power some more juice, making his signature fill the stone-walled corridor. The scent of a rainstorm surged, along with the roar of a river and the taste of aged rum. His aura flared a bright white, nearly blinding, and the woman gasped, stepping back.

She dropped into a low bow. "Your Holiness."

Oh, hell yeah.

I was damned glad this was working, because I really didn't want to fight someone as powerful as her.

"I am here to inspect your vault of treasures," Declan said. "I've an arrangement with Baphomet."

Ah, smart, to namedrop the holy figure whom the serving girl had mentioned.

"Baphomet." She whispered the word reverently.

This lady was so high on Declan's angel dust that she definitely wasn't thinking straight.

Perfect.

"I trust that no one has preceded us here?" Declan asked.

Ah, he was inquiring about Acius. Had the fallen angel beaten us to our target?

Please no.

"No one." She said the words with such vehemence that I grinned. I liked a woman who took her job seriously.

"Good." Declan gestured to the door. "Step aside."

"Of course." She stepped back and pushed open the door. Magic popped in the air, the charms deactivating, and Declan swept through.

I kept ahold of his shirt and followed, carefully keeping my footsteps silent. We *so* did not need Wally to show up right now, looking like a little feline slice of hellfire and brimstone. Worse, he'd probably crack a joke that she could understand and offend her.

Her gaze burned into my back as we walked down the wide stone-walled corridor. She couldn't see me, but I felt it all the same.

Finally, the door shut behind us.

I sagged with relief and let go of Declan's shirt. "Thank fates that's over."

"I thought it went well." He called upon his magical signature, dampening it.

It was a good plan. Whatever was coming at us down this corridor, we didn't need to announce our presence.

6

As we made our way through the underground Templar caverns, the stone-walled corridor gradually dipped down lower into the earth. It gave way to natural rock walls, until we were in a tunnel made of undulating rock formations. The torches disappeared in favor of pure darkness.

Declan raised a hand and let a ball of heavenly light form in his palm. It was intensely bright, shining light over the crazy rock formations that popped up throughout the tunnel.

"Given how far we've walked, we're probably outside the castle walls by now," Declan said.

"And at least a couple hundred feet underground."

The deeper we went, the farther we left any sight of human influence behind. The tunnel twisted and turned, and the air grew stale. The ground beneath our feet was covered in a fine gray dust that was marred by the footprints of those who had come before.

Wally appeared next to me, his smoky form looking right at home in the creepy tunnel. *So I hear we're going to see Baphomet?*

"I think so." I wracked my mind for any memory of the

name. "But it's strange that Templars would have any association with Baphomet. Isn't he the evil goat god that the Satanists worship? Something along those lines?" I knew I was probably slightly off on my religious knowledge, but that was the only figure I associated with that name.

Oh, he's no goat. The goat interpretation came later. Baphomet is something else entirely.

"What is he?"

You'll see. Wally shot me a toothy grin, which was actually kind of scary, given his fangs. He trotted off down the corridor, a real pep in his step.

"Did you get an answer from him?" Declan asked.

"No. He's excited to meet him, but didn't clarify what he really is."

Finally, we entered a massive cave deep within the earth. The ceiling soared hundreds of feet overhead, so high that Declan's light barely reached it. The space was entirely empty except for a statue in the middle.

It looked like a huge cat, sitting straight upright, with three faces. One faced forward, the other two to the left and right. Wally sat at the base of it, looking up. The statue had to be thirty feet high, and painted a jet black.

I joined him. "This is unexpected."

Wally looked up at me. *Not bad, huh?*

"No. Better than a Satanic goat god."

"We don't know that," Declan said. "Cats are tricky."

He's right. Wally rubbed himself against Declan's leg, apparently taking his words to be a compliment. *But Baphomet is the only way to get to what you seek. He guards his treasures like a cat. Very well.*

"Then we need to wake him up. Or call him to us." I inspected the statue for a clue. Some words were inscribed at the base, so I knelt to peer at them. "Should we recite these? *If* we could read them."

"Let's try." Declan knelt beside me so he could read the words as well. "I take that back. Those aren't even letters I recognize. What is that language?"

An ancient dialect of the Templars.

I looked down at Wally. "How do you know that?"

Please. I know things. Plus, me and Baphomet go way back.

My brows rose. "Does that mean we have an in with him?"

Wally shrugged. *Maybe. Not sure I'm his favorite hellcat, but he doesn't hate me as much as most.*

"Ah, that doesn't sound great."

Hey, he doesn't see me for the glorious hell beast that I am.

"Well, I do." I turned back to the statue. "What is he, anyway? A god?"

Wally shook his head. *Not a god. Not quite an angel like your guy over there. A religious figure. Like a talisman, or guardian of sorts.*

"Cool. Now help me wake this sucker up."

Wally recited the words at the base of the statue, sounding pretty fluent as far as I could tell. I mimicked the noises, and Declan mimicked me, since he couldn't hear Wally. It was obvious that neither of us had any idea what we were saying. It took us a few tries, but eventually, magic sparked on the air.

We kept going. The magic vibrated harder and harder, making my hair stand up on end and my muscles tremble. I shared a glance with Declan.

He gave me a look that suggested he agreed with me—this was a bit weird.

Finally, the huge stone cat shifted. His massive head creaked as he turned to look at us, the three faces shifting. Power rolled out from him, so strong that it nearly knocked me on my ass. His huge green eyes landed on Wally.

"Wallace of Helltavia, Son of Gorgora the Dark, Devourer of Souls, and Stalker of Nightmares. What are you doing here?" Baphomet's voice rumbled through the cavern. There was a hint of annoyance to it that almost made me grin.

Baphy! How are you?

Baphomet scowled. The face on the right hissed. I could only see it in profile, but the noise was unmistakable.

I looked down at Wally, murmuring out of the corner of my mouth, "I don't think he likes that name."

"Who are your guests?" Baphomet asked as he turned his attention to Declan and me.

This is Aerdeca and Declan. They seek to save their town of Magic's Bend, across the great ocean.

Baphomet tilted his head as he looked at us. "Tell me more."

I tilted my head to make sure I met his three sets of eyes, each of which landed on me with fairly regular frequency as he turned his head. "A fallen angel named Acius seeks to kill all of those in my town."

I explained what I knew of Acius in as much detail as I could, including the fact that he wanted me on his side. I didn't reveal that I was a Dragon Blood, but I implied that I had great power. Baphomet might know what I was anyway.

The giant cat listened carefully as I spoke, nodding occasionally. Once I was done, he spoke. "I see. This is very compelling. The gem has been held by the Templars for centuries, protected here beneath the earth. But you believe that this Acius could reach it."

"I think so. But he hasn't been through here yet, has he?"

"He has not."

Baphomet's words made hope spike in my heart. Yes. I could work with this. "Then please, let us pass. We can bring it back once we've stopped Acius. We don't want to raise the snake for our own, but we want to protect the stone from him."

"Clearly its location has been compromised." A look of distaste crossed Baphomet's features. "Loose-lipped humans."

Wally shook his head, as if he agreed.

"You may pass," Baphomet said. "But only if you prove yourself worthy."

"How do we do that?" I asked.

"This way." Baphomet grinned a Cheshire-cat smile.

My mind went fuzzy, and the earth dropped out from under me. My stomach lurched into my throat, forcing loose a scream. I clawed at the air as I fell, wind tearing past my hair and making my eyes water. Eons passed until I finally slammed into some water. It closed over my head, and panic flared.

No. Focus.

I was good in the water. I loved it.

Not under these circumstances, but I wasn't going to let it make me lose my mind.

I kicked for the surface, putting as much power into my movements as I could. Something twisted around my ankle. A weed.

I had the briefest flashback to my time in the Bermuda Triangle, when the terrifying weeds had wrapped around me and dragged me down. Lungs burning, I called a blade from the ether and bent over, slicing at the vine. Finally, I broke free and kicked upward. Another vine got me, then another, but I managed to cut them loose. My heart thundered and fear propelled me as I swam harder than I had in my life.

When I burst through to the surface, I sucked in air, gasping, and dragged my arm over my eyes.

Vision clear, I looked around, my heart thundering in my ears. Iron gray waves crashed into each other, and rain pounded down from steely clouds. Huge droplets landed in my eyes, nearly blinding me.

Then I heard the voice.

"Aeri!" Mari screamed.

I whipped around, kicking in the water to turn a full 360 as I searched for my sister.

"Mari!" I screamed so loudly that my throat immediately became raw. But I kept screaming, listening for a few seconds after every shout to see if I could hear her voice.

Finally, I heard it. I kicked hard toward the sound, using it as a guide.

A light in the water to the left caught my eye. Somehow, I knew immediately that it was a box containing all the secrets of my world. It glowed with the light of knowledge. It contained answers to all of my problems, solutions to how to handle my Dragon Blood magic and make my life easy and perfect.

Fates, I wanted it.

Desire like I'd never known clawed at me.

This was Baphomet's magic. It had to be.

The thought faded as the magic in this place overwhelmed me.

"Aeri!" Mari's voice drew my attention from the box, which was very slowly sinking to the bottom of the sea.

I kicked away from it, following my sister's voice. I'd come back for the box once I had her. Swimming to it now would take too much time. I couldn't afford to waste even a second when I still didn't know where she was.

A weed wrapped around my ankle, and my stomach pitched. I bent over to reach it, forced to duck my head underwater and hold my breath as I sawed it off my ankle. Finally free, I popped upright and gasped.

If this place was anything like the Bermuda Triangle, it was full of sharks.

As if one had heard my thoughts, I spotted a distinct gray fin pop out of the water about fifteen feet in the distance. It disappeared beneath waves, then reappeared like a nightmare.

Shit.

Sharks don't hunt people. Sharks don't hunt people.

Repeating the fact about sharks' natures didn't convince me that I wouldn't be the one to bump into a confused shark who tried to take a bite to figure out if I was tasty.

I ignored it, gripping my blade tight as I screamed for Mari again. Where the hell was she?

Splashing sounded from my left. My heart leapt, and I looked over.

A man struggled to stay afloat, his heavy clothes dragging him down. A droopy black mustache framed his mouth, and black eyes met mine.

Snakerton.

The black magic dealer from Blackburn Alley, the creepiest part of Darklane. He was a nemesis of mine, a guy who just plain sucked.

I hated Snakerton.

He screamed, thrashing in the water.

He was drowning.

Shit. Triple shit.

Just beyond him, I spotted Mari. She was going down too. And the box was still just out of the corner of my vision.

No way I was getting all three.

But I had to get two.

I couldn't just leave Snakerton, no matter how much I hated him. He sucked, he did things that were wrong. But he wasn't outright evil. And if I could save him...

I kicked toward him, ignoring the shark and shouting, "Keep kicking, Snakerton! Don't give up!"

As if to spite me, his head dipped below the surface of the gray water. In the distance, Mari struggled to stay upright as well.

They're probably fighting the weeds.

Of course.

"Mari!" I shouted.

She looked toward me, her dark eyes bright above the surface of the water.

"Catch!" I chucked her my knife. I knew she could handle herself. I wasn't so sure about Snakerton.

She reached up, somehow managing to grasp the knife by the handle instead of the blade, then ducked low, no doubt to cut the weeds that were probably wrapped around her legs. I called on another knife, drawing it from the ether, then kicked hard toward Snakerton.

He'd popped to the surface, gasping, his eyes narrowing on mine. "Aerdeca?" Annoyance flickered in his tone.

"Yeah, pal. Your only hope."

He choked on some water as he disappeared below the surface , then appeared again just as I reached him. "Bitch."

Seriously?

I ignored his words and dived beneath the waves. As I'd expected, vines twisted around his legs. I sawed them off, then pushed toward the surface.

Snakerton was still splashing around like an idiot, barely able to stay afloat.

"Can you not swim?" I demanded, my voice so cold that the water around us could freeze. My gaze moved toward the glowing box that held all the answers to my problems.

Damn, I wanted that box.

"Not well!" His head went under again.

Not at all, more like.

Vaguely, I recalled that I was here as part of a test to prove myself, but the thought was gone almost as quickly as it had arrived.

I grabbed Snakerton around the chest and hoisted him up so

his head was above water. "Just chill out or you'll take us both down."

"You suck at this."

"I hate you."

I dragged Snakerton along as I swam toward Mari, who was still struggling with the vines.

"Are you okay?" Seawater filled my mouth as I shouted.

"Almost!" She ducked below again to saw at the vines.

A shark circled in the distance. Holy fates, this was just too much.

How the hell were we even here? Mari and I could get ourselves into this kind of situation, but not Snakerton. And not some magic box that held the answers to all my problems.

Hang on a sec...

In the back of my mind, images of Baphomet flickered. The huge cat statue had come to life and told me to prove myself worthy. Then my mind had gone to fuzz and I'd dropped into this hellish ocean.

A test.

This was a test.

Which meant it was magic.

Snakerton thrashed in my arms, and the shark circled closer. Mari dipped below the surface again.

Was she really here or was this a mirage?

Only one way to find out.

I called upon my nullifying magic, allowing it to expand within me before shoving it out into the ocean. Snakerton continued to thrash, and I didn't dare let him go in case he was real and not made of magic. The moron would sink in an instant.

Fear chilled my skin as the circling shark neared. I grabbed for Mari as she went under again, never once letting up on my magic as I tried to nullify whatever spell had put me into this crazy realm.

I just had to kill all the magic in my surroundings and maybe this horrible place would disappear. Waves crashed over my head and water stung my eyes as I worked, wringing out every last drop of power from my soul.

Gradually, the waves calmed and Snakerton's struggles eased. Was he unconscious?

The glowing box caught my eye again. It was closer this time, sinking lower. Almost out of reach.

If I dropped Snakerton, I could grab it...

No.

I couldn't. I didn't know how this test worked, but if there was even a chance that Snakerton was real, I couldn't let the bastard drown.

Mari had things under control now that she had a knife, but worry seethed inside me. Exhaustion pulled, but I kept forcing my nullification magic into the water. Mari's head burst through the surface of the water and her eyes caught mine, then she disappeared in a poof.

The waves ceased entirely and the rain finally stopped. Snakerton disappeared in a flash, and the box blinked out of existence.

A half second later, I crashed to the ground, soaking wet. Coughing, I struggled upright, blinking the water out of my eyes.

I was back in the cavern. The massive ceiling soared overhead.

Wally stared at me. *You look like shit.*

"Thanks, pal." I looked up at Baphomet, who stared down at me with an unreadable gaze.

The huge black cat blinked, then tilted his head. "You did well."

I struggled to my feet, muscles still aching. "Hell of a test."

"I'm good at them."

"You sure are."

He waved his paw over me, and the water soaking my clothes evaporated in an instant.

"Thanks." I thought back to the glowing box. "That box was real, wasn't it? You put the answers to all my problems in there, then made me save an asshole and watch all the answers drift away."

"Yes."

I sighed wistfully. That box would have been nice. "Good choice with Snakerton. I hate that son of a bitch."

Baphomet smiled, an enigmatic cat expression. "He was only part of the test. The other part was that you used your magic to get out of it. Worthiness in this endeavor is not just worthiness of your soul, but also your skills. You are strong."

I'd gotten that strength the hard way, but I didn't share. He probably already knew.

I turned, searching for Declan. When I didn't see him, anxiety leapt in my chest. "Where is Declan?"

As if he'd heard me, the fallen angel hurtled down from the ceiling, his wings flared wide and his face blackened with smoke. He landed hard, going to his knees, and I hurried to his side.

He reeked of smoke, and I wrinkled my nose.

When he looked up, his frantic gaze found mine. He cupped my cheeks in his hands. "You're all right."

"Yeah. Yeah, I'm fine." Understanding dawned. "Was I in your challenge?"

"I had to save you." He surged to his feet and pulled me upright, dragging me into a hard hug. "Thank fates you're all right."

I squeezed him back, wondering what he had seen. Whereas

I'd gotten a water challenge, Baphomet had clearly stuck him in a burning building or something.

We pulled back from each other, and Declan gave me one last look. The worry faded from his face, and his expression cleared.

He turned to Baphomet. "Good one, cat."

Baphomet inclined his head. "You did well. Both of you have passed."

"Thank fates." I was ready to get ahold of that gem and get the hell out of there. We'd beaten Acius so far, and I wanted to keep it that way.

"Don't be so excited. You aren't nearly there, yet," Baphomet said.

"No?" My shoulders sagged.

"You've proven yourself worthy to me, but there are still challenges to be faced." Baphomet turned and raised a paw.

Magic surged on the air, and an ephemeral, sparkling veil fell away from the enormous cavern. It was the same size and shape, but now, I could see hundreds of treasures tucked into every crevice. Sparkling jewels, ancient books, enormous swords, and golden robes.

"Wow." I stumbled back, my eyes wide. "This was here the whole time?"

"Indeed it was. But the treasure you seek is so valuable that it is deep below this room." He inclined his head, nodding toward another tunnel that I hadn't seen before. It must have been hidden by the veil. "You will take that path, but you must show the same qualities you exhibited in your test, or you will never make it."

"I can do that."

Declan nodded his agreement.

"Then you may continue on with—"

A muffled sound of an explosion was accompanied by the earth shaking beneath my feet. I stumbled, grabbing onto Declan for support.

Baphomet hissed. "Someone has broken in. There is an intruder here. A powerful one."

7

PANIC FLARED IN MY CHEST. "ACIUS."

"Where is he?" Declan demanded.

"Deep below, someone is breaking their way through the catacombs." The cat's green eyes moved to mine. "I don't know how he found it, but there is a series of tunnels in this mountain. They aren't connected to the chamber containing the gem, but they could be."

"If you used the right amount of explosives." *Shit.*

"Precisely." Baphomet stared hard at us. "You must hurry. I cannot leave this room to defend the treasures. The tunnels are too small for me. You must stop him."

"We will." I gave the cat one last look, then raced toward the tunnel exit, Declan at my side.

"Remember!" Baphomet shouted. "Be as you were in the challenge."

Another blast rocked the ground beneath my feet. I stumbled, then righted myself, sprinting for the tunnel.

Declan and I raced through the smaller tunnel, leaping over rock formations and dodging boulders that stuck out of the walls. A faint light shined from the ceiling, a magical glow that lit our way. Explosions shook the tunnel around us, an ever-present reminder of Acius blasting his way to the gem alongside us.

Wally was nowhere to be seen, but I knew he'd show up when he was needed.

We'd run at least a quarter mile when the tunnel widened in front of us. The ceiling rose up and the floor dipped down. Murky water filled the lower section of the tunnel, rippling and bubbling for at least twenty yards ahead of us. A fanged fish leapt into the air, snapping its jaws.

"Fantastic." I looked at Declan, who was already flaring his wings wide. "Any chance I could get a ride?"

"Anytime." He held out his arms, and I leapt into them.

He launched us into the air, flying over the flooded tunnel floor. A fanged fish leapt high, aiming for us. The little beast clamped its jaws around my boot, and I kicked hard, dislodging it. The fish flew through the air and crashed into the water.

Another leapt toward us, and I called on a bat from the ether. I leaned over in Declan's arms and slammed the bat into the fish.

"Nice one."

A third fish jumped, then a fourth. A fifth, sixth, seventh. Declan began to fly in a complicated path, dodging left and right to throw the fish off.

It helped, and I took out the closest ones with my bat. A particularly wily bastard managed to clamp onto my ankle. The leather of my boot stopped his fangs from fully piercing, but fates, did it hurt. I tried kicking him off, but he was lodged firmly, so I swung my bat for more of the little bastards.

Finally, we reached the other side. Declan landed with a thud, then let me down and knelt, prying the fish off my ankle and tossing it back into the water.

An explosion rocked the cavern, and dust fell from the ceiling.

"Shit." I looked up, apprehension chilling me as I considered the fact that Acius could unintentionally bring this place down around us. "Thank fates he doesn't know we're here yet."

"If we're fast enough, he'll never know."

"I like the sound of that."

We set off again, sprinting through the tunnel. My lungs burned as we raced deeper and deeper. Now that I knew what this stone was capable of, I couldn't blame the Templars for hiding it so far beneath their castle. But damn, this sucked.

The tunnel opened into another cavern. This one wasn't nearly as big as the one in which we'd found Baphomet. The ceiling was far lower, but it was very wide. The strangest thing was the skeletons.

I didn't stop to inspect them, but out of the corner of my eye, I spotted at least a dozen of them, appearing to hold up the roof of the cavern. Their bleached bone arms were stretched over their heads, their hands propped on the ceiling above.

Weird.

"Help us." A voice drifted after me as I ran from the cavern. "Help us."

I stopped dead in my tracks, and Declan nearly slammed into me. He skidded to a stop, his hands coming to rest on my back. "What's wrong?"

"Do you hear that?"

"Hear what?"

"Help us," the skeletons said.

"There it goes again. They're saying *help us*." I hurried back into the cavern, keenly aware that we didn't have a lot of time to spare.

Twelve skeletons stared back at me, their heads twisted to face me. Each of them supported the weight of the cavern.

"Did you guys just...talk?" I asked.

"Help us." The voice came from a skeleton to the right. The jawbone didn't move, but I could hear the request clear as day.

"Are you stuck holding up this ceiling?"

"We are. We've been here hundreds of years. The Templars put us here."

"Prisoners?" I asked.

"Yes. We worshiped the wrong god."

Wasn't that how it always went? But could they be tricking me? Would they attack if I helped them?

Carefully, I studied them. I was good at reading people's intentions. It was a hell of a lot harder here, since the skeletons had no faces and not very much magic. But I sensed no ill will or trickery.

I translated the problem for Declan.

"Can't they just let go?" Declan asked.

The skeletons didn't answer, and I assumed they couldn't understand him the way they understood me. Probably the ghost power that I'd created and then modified for my own use.

"Can't you let go?" I asked.

"If we do, we'll be crushed before our spirits can ascend to the afterlife. Then we'll be trapped forever."

"So you've been waiting all this time for someone to come help you?" An explosion punctuated my words, a reminder that Acius was currently racing toward the gem, and he probably wasn't stopped by a band of skeletons.

"I'd like to say we don't have time for this," Declan said. "But I can see how that's not an option."

"Fates, it really isn't." The gem that we sought would help save hundreds of lives in Magic's Bend. But these skeletons had sentient souls that had been tortured for hundreds of years down here, trapped in the dark.

They weren't any less valuable than the people of Magic's

Bend. And there was nothing to say that we couldn't save *both* groups. There was no way to know how close Acius was to the gem, but I couldn't just leave these people here.

I wasn't going to choose one group of lives over the other.

My gaze raced around the cavern, searching for something to hold up the ceiling. There were massive boulders tumbled around that looked promising.

"If we pile up those boulders in a few places to support the ceiling, do you think that would work?" I asked.

"Yes, try," said one of the skeletons. "None of us could ever let go of the burden in order to attempt that, or we would all be crushed."

"We'll do it." I looked at Declan.

He didn't need me to say it twice. He swept into action, moving so fast he was nearly a blur. The boulders were light as air in his hands, or so it seemed. I joined him, moving as fast as I could through the cavern, gathering the boulders and piling them up. Thank fates for my superior strength, or it would have taken ages for Declan to do it alone.

My heartbeat thundered and nerves skittered inside me as I worked. I could just imagine Acius getting closer and closer to the gem as we piled rocks.

Sweat poured down my skin and my muscles ached, but finally, we had six sturdy pillars built of boulders.

I looked at the skeleton who I thought did the talking, even though I'd never seen his mouth move. "How strong are you? Do you think six is enough?"

"I believe so, yes."

I took his word on it. We didn't have a lot of time to debate, anyway. And without knowing how much rock was really above us—a hell of a lot, I was sure—there was no way I could do the math anyway. Not that I was a structural engineer.

For good measure, I stepped back into the exit tunnel.

Declan followed. If this cavern went down, we couldn't afford to get crushed.

One, I wasn't ready to bite it yet.

Two, Magic's Bend was counting on us.

"Okay, let go." I held my breath.

The skeletons lowered their arms.

The earth shifted, creaked, and groaned. Every inch of my body tensed. The skeletons paused, and if they'd had eyes, I'd have sworn they were wide.

The ceiling of the cavern settled onto the rocks but didn't collapse.

Thank fates.

"We've got to go," Declan said.

"Bye, guys. Good luck getting out of here." I spun to go.

"Wait. We can help you."

I turned around to face him. "How?"

I heard Declan stop moving down the tunnel. He returned to join me. He could only hear my half of the conversation, but he wasn't about to ditch me.

"Shortcut."

"That would be helpful." I translated for Declan, then stepped back and gestured to the tunnel. "Lead the way."

"I'll take the lead." A skeleton stepped forward. "The rest will follow."

An explosion rocked the earth around us, the muffled boom sounding from ever closer. We were nearing the gem, but so was Acius.

"Hurry," I said. "An evil fallen angel wants the stone of light for himself."

The skeleton nodded, then took off. His bony feet clacked against the stone ground, but he was fast. We followed, Declan and I side by side with a small army of skeletons trailing behind.

The rattle of their feet and bones was eerie, but we were so far past normal down here that it didn't faze me.

Within a hundred yards, we reached a division in the path. I'd have had no idea which way to go, but the skeleton in the lead didn't even hesitate. He veered right and picked up the pace. About fifty yards down, he stopped and dropped low, then scrambled into a little tunnel that was no more than two feet high.

"Seriously?" Declan asked.

"Man, I hope he's right." I dropped onto the hard ground and crawled after the skeleton. Claustrophobia set in immediately, but I shoved the fear aside and kept going, my eye on the skeleton's bony butt.

Probably wasn't considered a butt at this point, but the proper name for the butt bone escaped me, so it would have to do. Declan grumbled from behind me, but he kept up without trouble. It was easy to hear the rest of the skeletons following, and our weird little army continued on.

Finally, we exited the tiny tunnel to a larger one. The lead skeleton ran forward, and I surged upright to follow. He was about fifty yards down when he ducked low.

"Keep your head down!" He patted the top of his skull. "Or you'll lose it."

That was enough for me. I ducked as low as the skeleton—lower, actually. When the first spike jutted out of the wall only six inches above the gleaming white skull in front of me, I gasped. I'd assumed something like this was coming, but it was impossible not be shocked.

More and more spikes shot out, all of them fierce and pointed. They thrust forward with such force that they'd have pierced my skull with no trouble.

For good measure, I dropped to my hands and knees and crawled as fast as I could. Adrenaline pumped through my veins.

An explosion shook the walls around us, and gravel fell from the ceiling. We were getting ever closer to Acius. Whatever magic he was using to blow this place to bits was seriously strong.

A massive wood spike shot out right over my head, so close that I could feel the whoosh of air. My skin iced.

"I hope you're right about this." My voice shook as I directed the comment at the skeleton ahead of us. I *really* didn't want the spikes to start shooting out from down low. Skewered on a spike in an abandoned Templar tunnel sounded like a real bad way to go.

"I am correct," the skeleton said. "I think."

"We helped build this," said a bone man from behind.

"Good enough for me," Declan said.

Finally, the skeleton ahead of me stood. For good measure, I remained ducked low for a few extra yards, then I straightened and sprinted to catch up. An explosion tore through the ground, making the earth to my right tremble harder than the earth to my left—at least, it seemed that way from the amount of rubble that fell from the ceiling above.

"The idiot is going to bring this place down around our heads," Declan said.

"With any luck he'll just crush himself, and we can call it good."

"Wishful thinking." There was a chuckle in Declan's voice.

"And I'm going to stick to it."

"We're nearly there," the skeleton in the lead said.

"Thank fates." I was ready to grab this gem and run.

A moment later, the skeleton skidded to a halt in front of me. The cavern opened up in front of him, wide and lit with a pale golden light. I stopped next to the bone man, staring out at the enormous cave.

It was about the same size as the one in which we'd found Baphomet, except this one was full of strange rock formations shaped like arched bridges of solid stone and pillars that looked like giant penises sticking out of the ground. Any laughing that I might have done was squashed by the sight of a huge explosion blasting through the far wall.

"Acius." Declan's tone was ominous.

The man himself stepped through the clouds of debris. His dark wings flared wide, each feather tipped with the ash of his fall.

From behind Acius, a horde of demons spilled out of the tunnel.

On the far wall between Acius and me sat a pedestal. A sparkling red gem rested upon it. We were equal distances from it, and we'd have to race each other to get to it.

The fallen angel's gaze went straight to the gem. A wide, evil grin spread across his face. He was so intent on the gem that he didn't even see me.

It wouldn't stay that way.

I sprinted into the cavern, Declan and the skeletons at my side.

The demons spotted us—or smelled us—and charged, trying to cut us off as we went for the stone. Acius sprinted ahead. Declan launched himself into the air, his wings taking him upward almost faster than I could process.

I raced for Acius, lungs burning. The natural construction of the cavern made it into an obstacle course. I leapt over a chasm and onto a stone bridge, heading straight for the enemy and the prize.

To my left, a skeleton ran over another bridge. He tore his left forearm off and gripped the bone like a weapon. At the far end of the bridge, he collided with a demon, swinging his bone like a bat and smashing the demon in the skull. The skeleton was so strong that the demon's head caved right in.

Holy fates.

Four more skeletons collided with demons, each of them using their own bones as weapons.

Hell yeah. These guys were good backup.

I neared the end of my bridge, still twenty yards from Acius. An enormous demon waited for me, at least seven feet tall and made of muscle on top of muscle. His skin was the color of burnished ocher and his eyes flamed blue. He raised a hand tipped with serrated claws.

I called upon my mace, drawing it from the ether. The chain felt natural in my hand, and I swung it in an arc over my head, getting up some good momentum.

The demon lunged for me, his knife-like claws swiping out. I leapt off the end of the bridge, avoiding his strike as I swung my mace at his head. The spiked ball slammed into his skull, sending blood flying. The weapon stayed lodged in the demon's cranium.

Damn it.

I dropped the mace chain, abandoning the stuck weapon. Pain in the ass, but sometimes it just happened. Normally I'd retrieve the mace, but there was no time to spare and I had another one stashed away if I needed it.

Two of the skeletons had intercepted Acius—they were fast on their bony legs. He was trying to fight them off to reach the gem, which was still a good fifty yards away from him. Declan was battling a set of flying demons with dark gray skin and hands that glowed with green flame.

To my left, Wally appeared. He went for the face—his signature move—breathing fire with a gleeful yowl. The entire cavern was a disaster zone of bodies and blood, with weapons and magic flying.

A fire demon with bright red skin hurled a blast at me, and I dodged, sliding along the stone ground and slamming into a boulder. I scrambled upright and drew a dagger from the ether, hurling it at his head. The steel sank into his eye, and he yowled, falling backward to thud heavily onto the ground.

In the air above, Declan continued to fight, diving low to grab demons as they charged me.

I sprinted past the demon's body, headed for Acius. He'd defeated two of the skeletons, who lay in a pile next to him. The bones were slowly shifting, no doubt trying to piece themselves back together, but it would take them a while.

I was twenty yards from Acius. Too far for my mace. I drew a dagger from the ether and hurled it at him. The steel flipped end over end, glinting in the golden light.

It plunged into the back of his thigh.

He roared and spun, his wings flaring wide. Power rolled out from him, a massive force that nearly sent me to my knees. I gasped and stiffened, standing strong. An evil scowl twisted his face as he searched for who had thrown the blade. But when his eyes widened on me, he smiled.

A shiver raced down my spine.

Declan swooped toward us and fired lightning at Acius. A bolt struck him right in the head. He shook violently, the lightning coursing through him.

Three of his minions raced toward the pedestal, going straight for the stone of light. There were even more of them between me and the priceless gem.

"I've got him!" I shouted at Declan. "Go for the stone!"

Declan's gaze met mine briefly, then he scanned the ground, taking in all the demons who were headed for our target. Declan was our only shot. I yanked up my invisibility hood for good measure, giving myself the advantage over Acius.

Finally, Declan nodded and flew for the gem. Another winged demon appeared out of the tunnel and flew for him. The two collided in a crash of wings and limbs, wrestling in the air.

I sprinted for Acius, drawing another blade. I hurled it at

him at the same time he shot a blast of electricity toward me. The energy collided with my blade, diverting its path so it missed my target. The bolt of lightning kept streaking toward me, so large that it slammed into me despite the fact that Acius couldn't even see me.

I flew backward, trying to muffle my cry. The burst of power made it feel like my insides had been pulverized. I slammed into a big body.

It had to be a demon, since Declan was in the air and everyone on my side was a skeleton. The creature grunted with surprise, grabbing me with its huge hands. Claws pierced my chest and side. A cry tore from my lips.

"The hood!" Acius shouted. "Get her hood!"

It took all my strength to struggle away from the demon, who reached out blindly, grabbing for whatever he could get ahold of. His hands landed right on my hood, and he yanked, tearing it off my suit.

My invisibility faltered, and I appeared. Visible.

Shit.

In all my years wearing that outfit, no one had ever snagged the hood. I didn't let them get close enough.

Blood dripped down my torso and onto the floor as pain surged from the puncture wounds. Acius grinned with malicious glee as he observed me staggering to the side. I drew my sword from the ether and turned in a quick spin, slicing off the head of the demon who had grabbed me.

The demon's ugly skull toppled to the ground with a splat, and I turned back to Acius right as he shot another blast of electricity. I dropped the blade and drew my wooden shield from the ether, getting it up just in time.

The energy plowed into my shield, sending me to my knees. My arms ached, but at least my insides didn't feel like mush. All around, skeletons fought demons. In the air, Declan grappled with two of the winged monsters—each demon nearly twice the size of him, with long claws and muscles that made them look like body builders who'd grown wings.

He was getting closer to the gem, though, and he was stronger than the demons, despite his size. Faster, too.

Acius, for his part, seemed more interested in me.

I crouched behind my shield, drawing another blade from the ether. A blast of electricity slammed into the wooden protection, and I stumbled back onto my butt. There was no point trying to run from the damned blasts—they were so big they'd hit me no matter what.

But it took Acius a few seconds to charge up, so I leaned out from behind my protection and threw my blade at him, then immediately drew another from the ether.

My last one.

He dodged the first, but I'd expected him to, so I threw the other one while he was still darting out of the way.

It slammed into his side, and he roared, his gaunt form stiffening as he yanked the steel from his side. I couldn't give him any time to recover, so I called upon my mace and sprinted for him.

I swung the spiked ball high, around my head so it would avoid the shield. Behind Acius, Declan lunged down from the ceiling, headed straight for the gem. Both of the enormous winged demons were on the ground, their bodies and wings broken by the fall.

Declan grabbed up the gem as I neared Acius. He reached into his pocket. Going for a blade, no doubt. I could dodge that. It'd probably hit me, but not a vital organ.

Acius had been so strong that last time, my mace hadn't incapacitated him. So I took a chance, dropping the shield and grabbing the mace chain with both hands, giving it all my strength as I swung it toward him.

The ball slammed into his side, and he grunted, going down. The spikes were lodged deep in his flesh. Dark eyes met mine triumphantly.

Triumph?

Shit.

He hurled a small potion bomb at me.

I was so close that I managed to dive right, but not far enough. The bomb exploded against my side, soaking me with liquid.

Had it been a blade, like I'd expected, it wouldn't have been fatal.

But this?

I touched the liquid with my hand, confused. It didn't burn or bite. But my mind fuzzed a bit, going woozy and strange.

Acius laughed.

I looked up.

That laugh.

I loved that laugh. My gaze snagged on Acius's face.

Why was I fighting him?

Something deep in my mind tried to scream at me. I could just barely hear the sound of it, but the words were indistinct. All I could focus on was Acius, and how I'd do anything for him.

"I have you now." His voice was low and pleased as he yanked the spiked ball out of his side and stood straight. Pain twisted his features, and blood dripped from the wound. He staggered toward me.

"Of course you have me now." The words felt strange on my lips, yet natural. Why wouldn't he have me?

I'd do anything for him.

8

Declan swept down from the sky, his form drawing my attention upward, away from Acius.

"Fight him," Acius said. "Get me the gem."

"Of course."

Huh? Did I just agree to that?

Why would I fight Declan?

Before I could ask, the angel swept me up in his arms and carried me toward the cavern's ceiling. My eyes moved to the gem in his hand, and Acius's words filtered through my mind.

I needed that gem. My gaze met Declan's. "You got the gem."

"I do. Now let's get out of here."

"No."

He frowned. "What?"

His right hand gripped me tightly around the waist, but his left was just looped under my legs, the gem clutched in his fist. It sparkled red and brilliant, and I grabbed it.

Declan tensed, confused, but he didn't have time to say a word. I chucked the gem down to Acius, a strange pain shooting through my head as it left my fingers.

I shouldn't have done that.

The faint thought was replaced by a cloying fog.

"What the hell?" Declan demanded.

I punched him in the shoulder. "Let go of me!"

"What?" His bewildered dark eyes met mine.

"Put me down!" I shrieked, looking back toward Acius, who now gripped the stone. Panic twisted inside me.

I was on Acius's side!

No, I was on Declan's.

What the hell?

Why did Acius have the stone?

I could barely make sense of my thoughts.

"What's wrong with you?" Declan demanded.

"No!" Confusion tore my brain apart, giving me the biggest splitting headache I'd ever had.

Declan landed on an outcropping of rock, high on the cavern wall. He set me down, gripping my shoulders tightly.

Down below, Acius shouted up, "Don't bother. She's mine now."

Declan's wide eyes went from Acius to me, sweeping over my form. They landed on my side, where the sticky liquid was soaking through my jacket and shirt.

"Shit." His tone was violent.

He yanked my jacket and shirt off in the flash of an eye. He was careful not to touch the liquid as he chucked it away. I'd never seen him move so fast. His gaze landed on my hand, which was stained blue from touching the liquid that marred my side. He jerked off his shirt, revealing a broad expanse of chest, and quickly wrapped the cloth around my stained hand, firmly binding it.

I struggled against him, but he moved impossibly quickly, and I was so confused it made it hard for me to act.

Out of the corner of my eye, I caught sight of Acius flying up toward us, his wings graceful on the air despite the damage they'd received during his fall. The red gem was nowhere to be seen.

I ran for him, heading for the edge of the little cliff upon which we stood.

"Oh no, you don't." Declan grabbed me around the waist. He swept me up in his arms, then lunged off the cliff, his wings catching the air.

He was faster than Acius, his wings more powerful. He swept away across the cavern. Acius roared, following.

"Winged ones!" Acius shouted.

I thrashed to get back to my master, fighting Declan's hold. My head ached like I'd been hit by a freight train. From the tunnel down below, five more of the enormous demons flew into the cavern.

Acius pointed toward us. "Get her!"

"Shit." Declan's violent curse sounded in my ear. Just briefly, I stopped fighting him.

Why would I fight him?

Then the fog returned. Of course I had to fight him. He was keeping me from Acius.

I thrashed and kicked, eying the demons who flew toward us. Each was twice the size of Declan, with iron gray claws that looked like they were made of pure, sharpened metal. Their gray skin was rough and their eyes blazed with fire.

Would they rescue me or kill me?

I winced. My head hurt so badly. I was so freaking confused.

Declan cursed. "We can't transport out."

I was vaguely aware of the protection charms around the place, but I couldn't understand why he would want to leave here if Acius was here. Was it because the murdery-looking demons were almost to us?

"I can explain to them that we're on Acius's side." I struggled in his grip, almost breaking it. He'd forgotten how strong I was.

"We're not." Anger and despair twisted his features.

The huge demons were almost to us. Declan had better put me down, or he was dead.

Instead, he dropped my legs and raised one fist high overhead. He gripped me tightly with one arm around my waist, sending pain spiking through the wounds in my side. I cried out, the agony briefly clearing my mind.

Oh fuck, we're screwed.

Declan's magic exploded out of him, an enormous bolt of energy that was the width of a freight train. It blasted through the cavern ceiling above, making the walls shake. Silence descended as the accompanying thunder deafened me. Debris rained down, then Declan surged upward, flying through the hole he'd blasted in the earth above us.

I shrieked, clawing to get back to Acius.

Declan gripped me with both arms, tight enough that I couldn't get away. He flew so fast toward the sky that my eyes watered. Ten seconds later, he shot through to the dark night above.

I looked down. A blackened hole led straight into the earth, down to the Templar's secret cavern that was overrun with Acius's army.

"I should be down there!" I shrieked.

"No, you shouldn't." Declan grunted as he dug into his pocket and took out a transport charm.

"No!" I reached for it, but he jerked his hand away, then tossed the charm in the air.

After a second, it exploded in a cloud of silvery gray dust. He shot toward it, just as the huge demons from down below made it out of the tunnel. Acius followed behind them.

The last thing I saw before the ether sucked me up was the rage twisting Acius's face as Declan dragged me away.

Seconds later, we landed on the street in front of my townhouse, falling in a tangle of limbs on the hard pavement. The familiar air of Darklane shot some sense back into me. I gasped, my mind clearing.

"He's enchanted me."

"No shit." Declan surged upright and dragged me to my feet.

The clarity faded almost as quickly as it had come, and I hissed at him, stumbling away. "You took me from my master!"

"The hell I did." He lunged for me, grabbing me around the waist and binding me to him. His bare chest was hot against my skin, and vaguely, I realized I was standing in the street in my bra.

I didn't care.

Declan managed to press the comms charm around my neck, igniting the magic. "Mordaca, get back to your house. Your sister is in trouble."

"I don't need her!" I didn't need anyone but Acius.

Declan gripped me to him, making sure to keep my bound hand covered in the fabric. He dragged me up the stairs to my apartment, and I shrieked.

Somewhere in the back of my head, part of me died inside—just a little. The scene I was making on my front step was *so not* the icy Aerdeca that I presented to the world. This was mortifying.

The thought faded as quickly as it had come. As soon as we reached the top of the stairs, Mari appeared.

There was another brief flash of recognition when I saw her, a clearing of my mind, then nothing.

"What the hell is wrong with her?" she demanded as she opened the door to the townhouse and hurried in.

"I don't know, exactly." Declan dragged me over the threshold. "Some kind of potion that creates a false allegiance to Acius."

"This way." Mari hurried toward our workshop, and Declan carried me along as I fought like a wildcat.

We entered to find Mari starting the magical fire with the dust that was stored over the hearth. She ran to the shelves. "I may have something to counteract it, but it would help to know what it was."

"There was some on her hand, and it's now staining the shirt I wrapped around it."

"That might do it."

Declan thrust me into a chair, then grabbed a length of rope that sat coiled on the side table. In the back of my mind, I knew it was enchanted to hold people as strong as I was.

I tried to stand, but he was too fast, tying me to the chair.

"Let me go!" I shrieked.

"Chill out," Mari said. "You're not yourself."

That was true. But I couldn't seem to fight the demon inside me. Sweat poured down my skin as I thrashed against the bindings. The cuts in my side stung fiercely, and blood poured sluggishly, thick and white.

Declan laid his hands on my shoulders, feeding his healing magic into me. I could feel his weakness—he'd used up nearly all of his magic blasting our way out of that cavern.

I gasped as the warmth and comfort flowed into me. For the briefest second, I felt connection with him. Weariness hit me like a truck. No longer manically propelled by Acius's black magic, all I could feel was a desire to hug him.

There was no time for that.

I met his gaze. "If you can't fix me, kill me."

"No." Horror sounded in his voice.

"Dream on," Mari said.

"I'm dangerous," I rasped. I was a fucking Dragon Blood, for fate's sakes, and the most evil fallen angel in the world had gotten his claws in me. "I can't fight him forever. You can't hold me forever."

"I can," Declan said.

For the briefest moment, I believed him.

But still...

Too dangerous.

It was everything I'd ever feared—getting caught like this. Even worse, I wanted to help Acius.

My wounds knit fully back together, and I sagged against the chair. The lack of pain allowed the demon to come back, encapsulating my mind once more.

I struggled and thrashed, nearly tipping my chair over. Through increasingly blurry vision—was I *crying?*—I spotted Mari mixing up a potion in a bowl. She knelt at my side, both of her hands encased in thick black gloves.

I needed to get the potion on her. Acius's will surged through me, and I tried to swipe at her. If I could enchant her like I was, then she'd also be on his side.

Oh man, this was screwed up. I was aware I was enchanted, but I couldn't freaking fight it.

"This is the worst," I groaned.

"I've got you," Mari said. She pulled the fabric off my hand and carried it to the bowl of smoking liquid.

She dipped the stained fabric into the bowl. Red and yellow smoke rose up and twisted in an elegant dance over the bowl, and I vaguely recognized it as a spell to determine what kind of magic was in the potion that stained the cloth.

I thrashed in the chair, trying to throw myself backward on the stone floor to break the wood. Then I could get up and lunge for her. Declan came behind me and wrapped his arms around my chest, careful to avoid my stained hand that was bound firmly to the chair.

"How are you coming over there?" he asked Mari.

"Almost there."

"You got anything you can put on her hand to get rid of the potion?"

"Only once I know what the potion actually *is*."

It felt like ages passed as she worked. Occasionally, I drifted back into consciousness, drawn out of my crazy shell by Declan's touch.

"Don't worry, I've got you," he'd murmur in my ear.

In those moments, I clung to him like a lifeline.

"I'm sorry," I said between gasps.

"Not your fault."

"Kinda feels like it is." I winced. "I threw him the stone."

The memory made tears sting my eyes. I'd actually *done* that.

"Okay, I've got it." Mari dropped down beside my chair and pinched my chin, then poured a sour liquid down my throat.

I sputtered and gagged, but almost immediately, the weird haze disappeared from my mind and my compulsion to tear off this rope and return to Acius faded. I slumped.

Mari poured the rest of the liquid all over my hand. "To neutralize the poison."

"Thanks." I shivered. Hazy memories of what had just happened flashed through my mind. "What the hell was that?"

"A *really* powerful compulsion charm." Mari held up the vial. "This stuff will neutralize it, but the stuff has a compounding effect. If he hits you with it again, you probably won't be able to shake it off."

"Not even with more antidote?"

"Maybe." She shrugged. "But it's iffy."

I dropped my head back, and it landed on Declan's shoulder. "Damn, this sucks."

"Can we take the bindings off now?" Declan asked.

Mari looked at me. "Can we?"

I searched around inside myself, but felt none of the pervasive reach of Acius's power. The memory made a shudder run though me. "Yeah, I'm good. But if I seem like I might be turning to his side, zap me or something. I can't let him get me."

"No kidding." Mari undid the ropes. "But we're not zapping you.

I sat upright. Every muscle in my body ached. "God, that hurts."

"What happened?" Mari asked. She walked to the sink and filled a glass of water, then returned to me.

I took it and chugged the liquid, washing down the sour taste of the antidote. This bastard needed to quit poisoning me. And the only way to get him to quit would be to kill him.

"We almost got the stone," Declan said.

"But I gave it to Acius."

Mari frowned. "Well, shit."

I spelled out the whole horrible ordeal for her, explaining how he'd been delighted to see me and had turned his attention entirely to me.

"He planned it," she said. "He didn't know if he'd run into you, but if he did, he wanted to be able to hit you with that potion."

"Smart bastard," Declan muttered. "He'd known she'd try to beat him to the gems, and that she'd probably have the resources to find them. So he was prepared."

"He wants me as badly as he wants Magic's Bend. As badly as he wants that damned serpent." Just the idea made my stomach turn.

"They're all tools to get to you, now," Declan said.

I met Mari's gaze. "He'll want you, too, if he figures out you're like me."

I'll never let him.

"He doesn't know," Mari said. "Not yet, at least."

"How did your search in the North Sea go?" I asked. We needed a win here, and finding the other gem before Acius did was just as valuable as finding this gem. Either one would stop him from raising the Great Serpent.

Maybe my mistake wouldn't kill us.

Mari heaved out a breath. "Good, I think. We've narrowed it down to a small area. There's an old oil rig we want to check out."

I frowned. "Old oil rig?"

"The North Sea is full of them. This one has been abandoned a long time and reeks of magic."

Declan grinned. "It's something, then. Though oil drilling is primarily the realm of humans."

"We think it's hiding something. Cass felt like it would lead to information."

"Her dragon sense is never wrong," I said. "Acius is wounded—it'll take him time to heal from the blow I gave him."

Mari raised her eyebrows in question.

"Mace, right to the side. A lot of damage."

"Good." Mari nodded. "That'll give us a bit of time to rest. To recoup our magic."

Declan dragged a hand over his weary-looking face. "Fates knows I need it."

I looked at him, remembering the massive blast of lightning that he'd shot from his fist. It'd plowed through hundreds of feet of rock. Lightning shouldn't even be able to *do* that. But what he had was more than just regular lightning. No wonder he was tapped out.

I struggled to my feet. "You can catch some sleep at my place."

"Thanks."

Mari looked between us. "See you in the morning. Bright and early."

The clock showed that it was nearly three a.m. We could rest for a few hours. It wouldn't be a lot, but it'd be enough. We didn't have time to spare, anyway. We needed to get on the road as soon as we'd recouped the minimum amount of our magic.

We split for the night, with Declan and me stopping by my kitchen for a quick bite. Wally joined us, looking a bit ragged after his battle down below the Templar castle. As we shoveled in food—I was too stressed to even look at the Cheetos, which indicated how screwed up I was—I thought about Acius. Every second, I thought about his pull on me. How it'd been impossible to fight.

I'd thrown away the lives of everyone in Magic's Bend when I'd tossed him that stone. Or at least, that's what it felt like.

"Hey, you doing okay?" Declan asked.

I swallowed and looked up. "Yeah. Yeah."

"You're not."

I shook my head, dropping it. "I'm not."

"Let's get cleaned up and rest. You'll feel better."

He wasn't wrong about that. A shower did have me feeling a bit better—physically, at least. But as we crawled into bed together and I laid my head on his shoulder, the memories returned.

"He'd completely taken over my mind," I said. "If he'd managed to catch me, I'd be his weapon right now. I'd do whatever he said. Make whatever magic he wanted."

"Your greatest fear."

"Yeah. Exactly. And it almost came true today." I laughed bitterly. "They say that facing your fear makes you less afraid of it. Well, I'm more afraid."

"I think that only works for ridiculous fears. Your fear is...valid."

"Valid." I swallowed hard and stared at the ceiling. I tried to focus on the heat and strength of Declan—anything to distract myself—but it didn't work.

"You're getting stronger with your power," he said. "Every skill you've made, you've used it well and wisely. You've grown it. You're strong enough to defeat him."

"But not strong enough to not fall prey to his potion." I needed something that would prevent his damned potion from impacting me. I needed to face him. To fight him. But if one stray potion bomb could turn me into a weapon, I'd lose. Everyone would lose.

"I vowed to make no more new magic," I said.

"That was when you weren't controlling your magic well."

He was right. My signature going out of control and alerting Acius to what I was had scared me straight. Except now... "I need something that will make me impervious to his potion."

"The nullifying magic clearly didn't do it."

"No. The nullifying magic is something that I do *to* something else. This was done to *me*. I don't think the nullifying magic works retroactively like that."

"At least, not in the version you currently have it."

"What do you mean?" I frowned up at him. His features were silhouetted in the light of the street lamps from outside.

"Back at the Templar castle, you modified the ghost magic by turning it into something that allowed the ghost to see me. Allowed you to talk to the skeletons, who aren't quite ghosts at all. Why couldn't you modify the nullifying magic as well?"

Was I really strong enough to modify the nullifying magic in a way that would benefit me but not hurt me?

Somehow, I doubted it. Playing with the ghost magic was one thing, but this was far more dangerous. Nullifying magic—if I had too much of it—could hurt me.

I had to try, though. Even if I doubted myself. Because I liked that idea a hell of a lot more than making entirely new magic that was meant to cancel out the effects of Acius's potion. I didn't want to do that again. Not if I could help it. I was downright scared of it, in fact.

But modifying the nullifying magic...

I sat bolt upright. "I have to try."

9

"YOU WANT TO TRY NOW?" DECLAN ASKED.

"Now. There's no point in facing him if I'm not immune to his power to control me."

Declan sighed, but sat up. "I agree. I want a nap, but this is more important."

"Way more important." I scrambled out of bed and threw on my white robe, then raced down the stairs.

The fire in the workshop was banked, and the air carried a distinct chill. I hurried to the mantel and grabbed the tiny pot of powder, then tossed it into the flames. They burst to life, warm and fierce. I set the pot back down and turned to face the wall of shelves.

Declan took a seat at the table. "Let me know how to help."

"Sure." I scanned the shelves, looking for a few potions that we had ready antidotes to. I needed to test this magic, which meant I needed a few tester potions. Ideally nothing too painful or embarrassing.

I grabbed four different-colored vials from the shelves, along with their corresponding antidotes. Then I took a seat next to Declan and laid them out.

I pointed to the first one, a glimmering navy liquid that looked like a night full of stars. "This one will put me to sleep for twenty-four hours." I pointed to the white potion in front of it. "That's the antidote."

He nodded, clearly getting the gist.

I went down the line, explaining each potion. There was a coughing potion, a truth-telling potion, and a binding potion that would stiffen my muscles. "I'm not sure I can handle more than four anyway. So here it goes."

Declan picked up the sleeping potion, and I sat back in my chair, closing my eyes and calling upon my nullification magic. I was exhausted, so it took a minute, but it flickered to life inside me. The faint spark was easy to pull upon now, and I focused on it, fanning it to a flickering flame.

Once it had expanded inside my chest, filling me with its power, I imagined changing it. Morphing it. This power would no longer just be something that I pushed out into people or things—it would protect me. I imagined it wrapping around me like a barrier.

This was actually the true nature of nullification magic. If I had the full power of a nullifier, no magic could impact me. But then, I'd also lose all my other powers since it would suffocate them.

So yeah, this would be tricky.

"Now." I nodded to the potion.

Declan dripped some onto my hand.

Blackness crashed into me.

I had no idea how long I was out, just that I felt the antidote on my lips at the same time consciousness pierced me. I gasped and sat upright.

"Didn't work." Declan and I spoke at the same time.

I tried again, doing my best to give it my all. This time, when Declan poured the potion over my hand, I began to cough uncontrollably. My shoulders heaved and my breath drew short.

Declan poured the antidote on my hand, and gradually, I stopped coughing.

The third time I tried, desperation fueled me. When Declan poured the truth-telling potion on me, I spit out the first words that came to mind. "I care for you. A lot. Like, I want to spend all my free time with you. Always. Maybe forever. Probably forever, actually."

My eyes widened at my babbling. I'd just said that. Which meant that I hadn't manipulated my nullification magic in a way that would repel the potion, because I'd have played that closer to the vest if given a choice. I was falling for him—hard—and somehow, that made me want to hide even more.

"I care for you, too." He frowned at me. "Does that mean the truth-telling potion worked on you?"

I nodded. "I'd have kept that a secret longer if I could have."

"I'm glad you didn't."

I smiled at him, but deep down, I writhed with discomfort. I did care for him. But I'd really spilled my guts. And I believed him when he said he cared for me.

But I hadn't been in a real relationship in...forever. I wasn't ready for this. I'd really prefer to avoid facing the truth of it for as long as possible, actually.

But Mari and I had invented a truth-telling potion that acted more like a Spit-It-Out potion that made you spill your secrets. And I'd been dumb enough to choose it for this test.

Chalk it up to lack of sleep.

I met his gaze again. "Here goes nothing."

One last time, I tried with my nullification magic. To be honest, I was as afraid of this magic as I was of my feelings for Declan. It'd been a gift that I could learn to control this power that repelled anyone who touched me. I'd seen what this magic had done when it was allowed unfettered access to a person's being—it stamped out all their other magic, and with it, their soul.

At least, that's what Cass had told me it felt like.

But I had to try.

I drew in a steady breath and then exhaled, imagining the nullification magic filling every inch of my body. It flowed into my molecules. Into my atoms.

When it filled me to the brim, I gasped, slumping over.

An emptiness like I'd never known spread through me. It carved out my heart. Carved out my magic. Every other gift I had felt like it was stamped down so deep inside me that it disappeared. I lost all will to move. To function.

Gasping, tears springing to my eyes, I lunged backward, nearly tipping over in the chair.

I couldn't give this power free reign. Not even to try to repel Acius's potions. It would devour me. Worse, I couldn't fight Acius with all of my other magic repressed. He'd take me down faster than a lion with a lame gazelle.

Fear slithered through me as I fought to shove the nullification magic deep down inside me.

But it only spread. The power was so great that it felt like it was devouring me. Panic threatened to overtake me. I wanted to curl up in a ball and scream.

No.

That would be the end.

I had to fight this. I had to *control* it. Just like I'd controlled the ghost magic that I'd modified. I was strong enough. I just had to do it.

I sucked in a deep breath and envisioned physically wrestling the nullifying magic back into submission. It was a monster in my mind, but I was bigger.

Sweat poured down my skin as I struggled. Finally, I forced it deep down inside.

Declan gripped my shoulders. "Are you all right?"

"Yeah." I gasped the word, tears still prickling my eyes. Stress or fear—I wasn't sure what they were from. Probably both. "I couldn't make it do what I wanted. It almost devoured me."

"That's okay."

I gripped his arms, looking at him, knowing my expression was desperate. "But it's *part* of me. And it doesn't do what I want. I hate that."

I shuddered hard at the memory.

"You held it back," he said. "That's enough."

"Is it? It doesn't feel like it is."

"It has to be," he said. "Because it's part of you. It's one of your beasts that torments you. We all have them—monsters from our past, magic we can't quite control."

"You have them?"

"Of course. Memories of battle? Losing friends? Those beasts rear their ugly heads whenever my guard is down. Leads to some pretty ugly nightmares."

I reached for his cheek, brushing my thumb over the firm surface as he spoke.

"We can't defeat all our beasts, but we can tame them. That's what you did."

I sucked in a deep, slow breath, focusing on his words. I liked the way he put that.

I nodded slowly. "I had to try. I'm glad I tried."

Because now I knew that I really was in control. Maybe I couldn't make the nullification magic do whatever I wanted—but I wasn't sure anyone could do that. But I could control it. I could keep it from overpowering me, even after I'd let it out of its cage. And I'd modified the death magic earlier today.

I was stronger than I'd realized.

Thank fates.

Because I was going to have to make *new* magic, no matter how much I didn't like the idea. Something that actually *would* repel Acius's potions.

Was I ready for that though?

After tonight, yes. I hoped so.

But I didn't want to think about it. Not quite yet.

Declan's touch was still warm on my arms, so I focused on that.

I clung to his touch like a lifeline. His mere presence fed warmth and light into me, and I drew on it.

I hated to lean on another person, but now I had to. Now, it was worth it. Now, I needed him.

Maybe that's what life was. Of course we all wanted to be totally independent and strong. But sometimes, we couldn't be. And if we could find someone who we didn't mind leaning on...

I gave a bitter laugh.

"What is it?" Declan asked.

"Oh, nothing. Just having some big life realizations here."

"Like what?"

I looked up at him. I'd just confessed to caring for him. I could tell him this.

But...

I wouldn't.

Not now. Not if I didn't have to. Maybe I was still playing it too close to the vest, but now wasn't the time. There'd be plenty of time later to talk about our feelings and my emotional growth from a frozen, wizened soul into a slightly less frozen one.

Anyway, I'd had a big enough night already.

"Nothing." I stood, pulling on his arm to make him rise. "Let's go to bed."

I followed him up to the bedroom, clinging to his hand the whole time. When he shut the door, I pretty much jumped him.

I tugged on his hand to spin him around, then threw myself into his arms. "Make me forget tonight."

I knew that having big emotional realizations about him followed by sex was probably a quick way to get myself even deeper into this thing between us, but I didn't care. I needed him. I wanted him.

He pulled me toward him and kissed me, driving away every concern in my head. Heat flooded me, filling up the empty spaces left by the nullification magic.

I drove my hands into his hair and held his head so I could kiss him until I couldn't breathe. He reached for my butt and gripped me tightly, hoisting me up against him. I wrapped my legs around his waist.

His hardness pressed into me, and I moaned. "Take me to bed."

He turned and walked toward the bed, laying me gently down on the mattress. He'd never put a shirt back on since his was stained with the potion that Acius had hit me with, so I ran my hands over his hard chest, down his waist, to the loose sleep pants.

My fingers fumbled with the drawstring, but Declan didn't care that I was clumsy. He just groaned and tilted his head down to kiss my neck. Pleasure shivered through me as he ran his tongue along the sensitive skin.

The rest went by in a blur of pleasure. By the time I passed out, I was so exhausted that sleep stole through me quickly.

Dreams chased on its heels—horrible dreams that spelled out my future in terms that were too clear to ignore.

I could become Acius's weapon.

With one well-placed potion bomb, he could make me his. From there, I'd do anything he asked. Visions of myself killing my family, my friends, flashed through my mind.

I could be forced to create an earth power that could destroy Magic's Bend from below.

I could be forced to use my power of suggestion to convince governments to commit genocide.

I could be forced to strike the entire world with lightning until I collapsed from exhaustion.

I was the most powerful weapon in the world—if I let someone use me like that.

I woke at six, gasping and tense.

Declan woke quickly, silently, and leaned over me. "Are you okay?"

I nodded, thinking about the dreams. To my practice last night with my magic.

It hadn't solved my problem. What it *had* done was make me desperate. There were two impossible futures that awaited me. Allowing my nullification magic to devour me so his potion bomb wouldn't affect me, or let him control me. I wouldn't—couldn't—live with either of them.

I was going to have to make new, permanent magic.

Hell, what was the worst that could happen in that scenario anyway? That people would figure out what I was?

That had already happened. Acius knew, and he was pretty much the scariest big bad that was out there. I didn't want the government to know about me, but right now, that was small potatoes compared to what I faced.

I had to take the risk.

I pushed Declan aside and sat up. "I know what I have to do."

He sat, looking at me quizzically. "What?"

"I need to create new magic. New, permanent magic. Something that will protect me against potions and other harmful charms. There has to be something like that out there."

"Like a shield."

I nodded. "Exactly."

"Let's hurry."

I took the fastest shower in the history of the universe, dressed in a fresh ghost suit—my only spare—then swung by my kitchen to grab a bagel. I needed some energy for what was to come. The thought made a faint shiver run over my skin, but I ignored it.

I'd be fine.

If last night had shown me anything, it was that this was necessary. I hurried into the workshop and found Mari there.

She turned to look at me. "You're going to make new magic, aren't you?"

"Something to protect me from his potions. I have to. If he hits me again, I'm on his side, no question."

She nodded, looking resigned. "I should, too, then."

"We're not confident that he knows you're like me."

"But I can still be used as a weapon to convince you to join him."

That was true enough. And Mari was a big girl. As dangerous as this was, I wouldn't want her to go through the agony of having her free will stolen. Those flashes of awareness that I'd experienced while being under his spell had been the worst.

"Let's find a power in the big book." I walked toward our bookshelf. "I don't want to wing this one. It has to be perfect."

All of the other magic that I'd created, I'd just envisioned. And I knew what I wanted with this new power, but it'd be easier if I knew of one that already existed. If I had a name for it and specific parameters to envision, it'd be easier and more likely to do exactly what I wanted it to do.

Our bookshelf was stuffed full of all sorts of old grimoires and magical tomes. Right in the middle sat an enormous leather-bound volume that was a compendium of most of the magical powers in the world. I pulled it down and blew off the dust.

"We really need to take better care of those," Mari muttered.

I winced and nodded, then set the book down on the worktable and flipped open the pages. The scent of old paper wafted up, and I inhaled. I liked the smell of books, even though I found less time than I'd like to read them.

Mari leaned over my shoulder, her ebony hair swinging free. She was dressed in her fight wear, but she hadn't pulled her hair back yet. It smelled of her shampoo, a light lilac scent that was so familiar.

Together, we scanned the pages as we flipped through them, trying to find the perfect magical gift.

Declan joined us after his shower. "How long until you're done?"

"Fifteen or twenty minutes." I wasn't sure about that, but we actually didn't have all that much time anyway. Depending on the magic he had at his disposal, Acius's wound could be healed by now. We needed to get a move on with the second gem.

"I'll be back." Declan left without another word, and Mari and I returned to our work.

A moment later, my eyes fell on a promising-looking power. I pointed to it. "Iron skin."

Mari squinted at it and read aloud. "'A person whose skin is impervious to all potions and concoctions that are intended to do harm.'" She grinned and met my gaze. "That's perfect. We don't want to mistakenly make ourselves immune to healing potions. With this, Acius can hit us with his controlling concoction, and it won't do a damned thing."

I continued scanning the text. "They're most commonly a type of supernatural from Africa, where potions are most common. Maybe a magical evolutionary trait?"

"Maybe. But it's about to be ours."

"Perfect." I snapped the book shut then returned it to the shelf. "Where should we do this?"

"In front of the fire?"

It was as good as anything else. The floor was smooth stone —easy to clean, which would make the blood a non-issue.

"Perfect." I knelt by the fire, which flickered warmly against my skin. My stomach turned a bit at what was to come. I was committed, but that didn't make the process any more pleasant.

Mari knelt next to me. We each drew a dagger from the ether.

I looked at her. "Ready?"

"Ready."

"Together." Briefly, I squeezed her hand, then sliced the blade over both of my wrists. Pain shot through me as the blood began to pour from my veins.

White liquid dripped to the ground, mingling with the black of Mari's blood. We'd never figured out why our blood was like this, and I had a feeling we might never know. *Just add it to the list of the other weird things about me.*

My head grew woozy as the blood flowed, and I gripped Mari's hand. She squeezed back. As the blood left my body, I began to pour out my magic as well, forcing it from my soul. Mari did the same, and her magic sparkled in the air around us.

Memories of when Aunt had forced us to do this together flashed in my mind, chilling my skin. I drew in a ragged breath, trying to force them away. My vision blackened at the edges, and I kept pouring my magic out of me. It drifted toward the blood on the ground.

I envisioned the power that I wanted, imagining potion bombs crashing against my skin and doing nothing to me. They were like water balloons, just a mild annoyance.

Iron skin.

That was exactly what I needed. I held on to the vision of the power, gripping Mari's hand tight as I began to sway, weak from blood loss.

I glanced over at her, horrified at the sight of her hollowed cheeks and stark eyes.

That's what I looked like.

Power never came easy.

My breathing grew shallow as the last of my blood and magic poured out of my body. My vision blackened entirely as my energy died.

I had no more strength. No more will. I was nothing. Just air.

Magic sparked around me, changing. Mutating. It crackled with power, bright and strong, then flowed back into me. Mari gasped, her grip tightening.

Strength flowed into me, flooding my muscles and veins. New magic crackled within me. My skin felt different. Stronger, somehow.

I gasped and opened my eyes.

"It worked." Mari surged to her feet with a burst of energy.

I joined her, nearly vibrating with pleasure at our success.

There were downsides to this, no question. But right now, I needed to focus on how this would help us. I'd deal with the consequences of learning to repress this new magical signature later.

For now, we were adding to our arsenal in the fight against Acius.

10

After testing our new magic with a freezing potion and determining that we were no longer susceptible to harmful magical potions, we quickly cleaned the blood off the floor. Declan met us a few minutes later.

I turned to Mari. "Where to?"

She'd said their clues had led them to the North Sea, but not where, exactly.

"We're meeting Cass and the Undercover Protectorate in Scotland. Cass has our ride, and Jude should have a map."

"Nice work."

She gave a wry smile. "We were busy. But I think we've narrowed the location of the stone."

"Perfect."

Mari looked at both of us. "Ready?"

I was dressed in my fight wear, and I'd had a bagel—plus the blood ritual to create new magic. "As ready as I'm ever going to get."

"Good enough for me." Mari held out her hands, and we each took one, gripping tight.

Her transport magic ignited, and the ether sucked me in and spun me around, then spit me out on a towering cliff where the wind bit into my exposed skin and the clouds hovered low.

My hair whipped around my face, and I pushed it back, turning to face Mari. "Northern Scotland?"

"Good guess."

It was where the Undercover Protectorate was located, and it was right on the North Sea. Not to mention, it looked like a Highlander would come striding over the green cliffs any moment.

The sea below smashed in iron gray waves against the rocks, and I studied it. "Somewhere out there, huh?"

"Not inviting, but yeah."

Magic sparked on the air next to us, and I turned to face it. Jude appeared out of the air, her dark braids whipping on the wind. The leader of the Undercover Protectorate grinned widely, her teeth perfectly white against her brown skin. Starry blue eyes met mine, then moved to Mari.

She shouted against the wind, "You been waiting long?"

"No. You've got the map?"

Jude pulled a folded piece of paper out of her pocket and handed it to Mari. "Florian found it in the library. I knew we had something that might help."

"Thank you." Mari nodded. "We owe you one."

"You don't." Her eyes turned serious. "And Cass explained what you're up against. If you don't get the gems and you need help, we're there. We're already working on a shield charm for Magic's Bend. It won't be able to stand against the Great Serpent forever, but it might slow him. We're gathering troops as well. Just in case."

"Thank you." The sound of a helicopter caught my attention, and I looked up to see one approaching our spot on the cliff.

Cass sat in the passenger seat, her red hair bright even from this distance. Next to her sat the captain, a brunette in her mid-sixties wearing badass sunglasses.

"That's our ride?" I shouted.

"Cass had a connection," Mari said. "Faster than a boat."

I nodded, stepping back as the chopper landed near us.

"Thanks!" Mari waved at Jude, then ducked her head and ran toward the chopper.

Declan and I followed, then piled into the little machine and buckled in.

The captain turned around and shouted, "I'm Nielson. You got a map?"

Mari leaned forward and handed over the folded piece of paper that Jude had given her. "That shows the location of known magical anomalies in this part of the North Sea."

Nielson nodded and studied the map, her lips pursed. "Any of them you want to check out first?"

Mari pointed to one, looking at Cass for confirmation. "That one, I think."

"That's the one," Cass said.

"We'll head there first." Nielson pinned it to the dash and grabbed the steering mechanism. "I'll have you there soon."

"Thanks!" Cass said, then turned back to us. "I've known Nielson a long time."

"You're always getting in trouble and needing to be bailed out," Nielson said.

Cass just laughed.

I met her gaze. "Thanks for the help."

"Anytime. My sisters were bummed they couldn't be here, but they're dealing with something pretty important."

"Pretty explosive, you mean."

She nodded. "An artifact imbued with magic that's decaying

faster than expected. If they don't find it in time, a whole town will go boom."

Yeah, that was some compelling stuff.

As Nielson piloted us away from land, I leaned over and looked down at the iron gray sea. Soon, we lost all sight of the green cliffs.

"Everyone, give me your phones," Cass said. "I'm programming Nielson's number into it in case you need it."

In case she didn't make it and we needed to call for our ride, was what she meant.

I handed over my phone, and she tapped the number in, then passed it back to me.

About forty minutes later, magic began to spark on the air.

"You feel that?" I asked Declan.

He nodded.

"We're getting close." Cass grabbed the map and looked at it, then showed it to Nielson. She pointed to a specific dot. "Go to this one. I think I'm getting the strongest tug from that direction."

Nielson turned the chopper to follow Cass's dragon sense. Between the helpful map and her power, I had a feeling we'd hit the nail on the head the first time.

A few moments later, a small blip appeared on the horizon. I squinted and leaned forward, pulling against the seat belt. "What is that?"

"An old oil rig." Nielson frowned. "Looks like it's been abandoned a while."

"Do they usually abandon oil rigs?" Cass asked. "Seems unsafe."

"Bad for the environment, at least," Declan said.

As we approached, the sense of magic on the air grew stronger. It prickled against my skin, making me feel intensely uncomfortable. Like we should turn around.

"Dead giveaway," I muttered.

"The repelling charm?" Declan asked.

"Yep. Sure, it works on humans. But it's like a beacon for supernaturals. *Good shit hidden here.*"

Nielson circled the rig so we could get a good look at it. The structure was complex. Huge, really. It bobbed on the surface, looking like a hulking beast of iron and rust.

"This is it," Cass said. "I'm looking for anything that can provide info about the gem, and my dragon sense is going wild here."

"We trust you." Mari turned to Nielson. "Can you drop us on it?"

"Can't land, but I can send down a ladder."

"Perfect."

Nielson hiked a thumb toward the back. "Under your seat. Tie it off to the rails."

Declan found the ladder under his seat and pulled it out, then opened the chopper door. Wind blasted in, whipping my hair around my face.

Quickly, he tied it off to the rails.

"I'm out." He looked at Nielson. "Thanks for the ride."

"Anytime, sugar." She winked at him.

He winked back.

My heart warmed.

Oh boy.

Now was *not* the time for that. How had I gone from deciding to try to control my nullifying magic so we could date to having real, solid feelings for him?

Feelings that actually scared me a bit.

Scratch that. Scared me a lot. A lot was the actual amount.

Whatever. These were intense circumstances. That totally increased the feelings of attachment, right?

I needed to get my head in the game. I had a job to do.

I moved toward the door and leaned out, watching Declan descend as I inspected the surface of the oil rig. We'd seen no sign of life, but that didn't mean that one wouldn't appear as Declan neared it.

"There are no guards," Mari said.

I directed my voice toward Cass. "Do you think you feel the stone here, or just information about it?"

"Both."

Thank fates.

But why were there no guards? There was no way the gem was just sitting around on an old abandoned oil rig.

Something was definitely fishy.

"You next, Blondie," Nielson shouted.

Normally, Blondie might insult me. But Nielson was so damned cool that it didn't even faze me.

"Thanks for the ride!" I lowered myself onto the swinging ladder, gripping the metal rungs tightly as the wind tore at my hair.

Far below, the oil rig bobbed. I had to be sixty feet up, probably more. As quickly as I could, I climbed down to the platform. The ladder swung wildly in the wind, twisting and turning more and more the farther down I got.

"Almost there!" Declan's shout carried up to me.

Thank fates.

This would give anyone a complex about heights.

My hands were nearly frozen by the time I was close enough to jump down. I let go and landed in a crouch, then stood. Mari landed next to me a moment later, followed by Cass.

The ladder disappeared—magic, no doubt—and the chopper whirred away. The four of us spun in a circle, inspecting our surroundings.

"There's no one," Mari said.

"It's a cover." I couldn't see every inch of the oil rig. It was like a weird little city in the middle of the ocean. But it felt so dead that it was clear there was no life here. "Let's search."

We spread out, careful to keep within shouting distance of each other, and began to search the rig. Salty sea air blasted past us as we moved throughout the labyrinthine structure. The repelling magic worked overtime, giving me the strongest sense of anxiety that this place was going to sink into the sea and take us down with it.

"Clever charm," Cass shouted. "Freaking hate them."

I rubbed my arm. "Feels so real."

The platform beneath me shook. I grabbed onto a big metal rail, clinging tightly. My friends did the same.

The platform tilted hard to the right. My stomach lurched. Magic flared on the air as water rushed over the surface of the platform.

Shit!

Were we going down?

Every instinct I had screamed to grab a transport charm and get the hell out of there. If something this big went under, it'd pull me down with it.

I sucked in a ragged breath, clinging tightly.

"What do we do?" Mari shouted.

Even though the ground beneath me looked tilted and the water rushed up over the sinking right side, I didn't feel gravity pulling any harder on me from that direction.

It should be dragging me toward the water, right?

"I think it's an illusion!" I shouted, my heartbeat slowing. "Keep searching!"

"There's something over there!" Cass pointed to an iron wall in front of me. "I can feel it!"

I was the closest one, so I scrambled forward, making sure to hold on to various metal posts and fittings as I went. Water rushed toward my boots as the right side of the platform dipped deeper into the water.

I couldn't figure out if it was illusion or real, so I ignored it. I needed to get to the weird wall that was covered with metal fittings. If Cass said there was something there, then there was. Her dragon sense was never wrong.

As I neared, I realized that the fittings were actually gears. Dozens of them in all sizes. Really old gears, actually. They were the rusted red color of iron that had sat too long in the sea air.

Anachronistic, really. They looked more like decoration than anything else, each one stuck on the iron wall behind it. The wall itself was about ten feet by ten feet. Some of the gears touched and some of them didn't. There was no point to a gear that didn't touch another gear, so why were they there?

Declan made it to my side first, then Cass, and finally Mari.

"It's something, all right," Cass said. "But I've no idea what."

The gears were distracting, but I moved my attention to the wall behind it. There were some spots that were worn smooth—almost like paths that connected the gears.

"Hang on a second..." I approached.

Declan joined me. "You're looking at the smooth paths, aren't you?"

"Yeah." I reached for a gear and tried to move it so it traveled over the smoothed path on the metal wall behind.

It did, and fairly easily. I moved it so the gear touched the other gear at the end of the path.

"I think it's a puzzle door," Cass said.

"Let's make all the gears touch," I said. "There must be a pattern that will make them operational."

Together, we moved the gears into position. It took a few tries to get the order exactly right, but as soon as all of the gears were touching at least one other gear, they began to move.

We stumbled back, giving the door some room to work. The

gears creaked into motion, spinning faster and faster until the metal wall began to rise.

I grinned. Definitely a door.

But it wasn't.

Once the door reached the top and clanged to a stop, the air around us shimmered. The oil rig disappeared. Suddenly, we stood in the middle of a bustling city street.

Except it was a city unlike any I'd ever seen.

For one, it looked like we'd gone back in time by about a hundred and fifty years. Probably somewhere in England. The buildings were all old brick and wood, smoke billowing from their chimneys and mullioned glass windows glinting dully in the faint light. The people were all dressed in old-time clothes that looked vaguely Victorian, with tailcoats on the men and gowns on the women.

Carriages filled the street, except there were no horses. Engines were strapped to the backs, crazy monstrosities made of iron and wood that belched steam. Actually, they weren't the only weird machines I saw. In the air, a hot air balloon floated. A weird motor was attached to that as well, along with a metal fan. A strange metal stomping machine belched steam as it compacted the trash in a bin on the street, and a street vendor strolled alongside a cart that walked on four mechanical legs. It also had a small steam engine on the back, though this one belched green smoke instead of white.

"Wow," Mari whispered. "It's like steampunk."

I eyed all the fancy, nineteenth century-style clothing that people wore. We probably stood out like sore thumbs. "Come on. We need to take cover."

I grabbed Declan and Mari, and Cass followed. We ducked into an alley, keeping to the shadows.

I peeked back out into the street, awe spreading through me. "It's a whole secret city."

"Frozen in time," Declan said.

"Hidden," Mari added.

"We need new clothes," Cass said. "I don't see anyone wearing anything modern."

The closest thing to modern was the menswear, since at least that wasn't a freaking gown, but even the guys were dressed in fancy woolen suits with a bunch of metal toggles and leather straps.

"I'll use illusion," Cass said. "That way we can still fight. Because no way I'm walking around a hostile environment in a corset."

Actually, I kind of liked the clothes. Not the colors. There was too much brown and gray and dark green. But the styles were pretty cool. Not that I wanted to fight in a corset and heavy skirts, like Cass had said. Though I did see a few women wearing cool trouser suits with knee-high leather boots and vests.

Cass's magic flared briefly, and I looked down. Yards of dark green fabric flowed around my legs. A leather corset studded with brass fittings wrapped around my waist, and a really impressive display of cleavage was framed by the high collar and tight sleeves.

I looked bad ass, but I felt like I was wearing my normal clothes.

Perfect.

Cass grinned at me. "I find that tits work well as a distraction."

I eyed hers, which were impressively displayed in a maroon version of a dress similar to mine. "I have to agree."

The corner of Declan's mouth quirked up in a smile, but he said nothing.

Mari wore black, as usual, and looked like a sexy steampunk

mistress of the dark. Compared to her normal Elvira dress, it was conservative, but she looked good.

Cass gave her a wry look. "I think your usual outfit would give these fellas a heart attack." She nodded toward the staid-looking men who strolled on the street beyond.

"Fair enough." Mari grinned.

Declan was dressed like one of the men, but his broad shoulders filled out his suit coat so nicely that I had to admire him. "You clean up nice."

He tugged on the leather vest that was decorated with tiny brass spikes. "Thanks."

I peered back out at the street. Heavy fog hung low over the city, a combination of the sea clouds and the thick smoke that wafted from the chimneys. We were still in the middle of the North Sea as far as I could tell. The bite in the air was the same, as was the faint scent of sea salt that fought its way through the smoke from the chimneys.

"So the gem is out there somewhere?" I asked.

Cass nodded. "Should be. I can feel it. Not exactly where, but it's close by."

"We'll have to find this the old-fashioned way." I eyed the street, looking for a bar. "Let's find someone important, and I'll get them to spill."

"What about that place?" Declan pointed to a fancy bar called the Steam and Whistle. There even looked like there was a bouncer outside.

"Perfect." I set off out of the alley, cutting across the street between steam carriages that trundled along the cobblestones, rattling away. The drivers all wore goggles, which seemed a bit excessive, but fashion seemed to be king here.

Pale orange flame glowed in gas lamps as we passed, sending dark shadows flickering over the ground. We passed by shops full of the usual potions and magical instruments, but also ones full of metal contraptions that did all manner of things—from boiling eggs to sewing buttons onto a suit. If it could be done by a steam engine, by Jove, these people were going to see that it was done.

I neared the bouncer at the Steam and Whistle. His muddy brown eyes fell immediately to my breasts, and I cleared my throat, giving him my iciest stare.

I'd use my suggestive magic if I had to, but I probably didn't.

"Well?" I imbued my voice with all the chill that I'd developed in my time as Aerdeca. "What are you waiting for?"

"Huh?"

Oh, he wasn't a bright one. "Open the door."

"Are you members?"

"Open the door." I added some disdain to the ice. "Of course we're members. I cannot believe that you are so incompetent that you do not recognize us."

My hard stare seemed to do the trick, and he turned to open the heavy wooden door. I sailed past him without an acknowledgment, into a bar that looked more like a mad scientist's laboratory. A wide wooden counter separated the barman and his wares from the patrons.

Behind the bar, dozens of long glass tubes bubbled with colorful liquid. Green lights surrounded them, accenting the drinks on and off. The rest of the space was lit by a warm golden light from crystal lamps that hung high overhead. The bar stools were upholstered in dark red leather, while the booths were black with crimson fittings.

Several of the booths sat on raised daises. "Perfect. Makes it easy to find the important people."

I turned to Cass. "You getting anything?"

"Give me a moment." She closed her eyes, her brow furrowing in concentration. "Okay, when I think about finding someone who might know about the gem, my dragon sense points me in that direction."

She nodded toward a back corner where there was a single raised table. An older man sat at it, a monocle stuck to his face and a contented smile pulling at his lips.

"Then that's my prey."

11

I TURNED TO MY FRIENDS. "WILL YOU GUYS ASK AROUND TO SEE IF Acius has already been here? I'm going to take care of him."

"Good plan." Mari nodded.

"Be careful," Declan said.

"Always." I swept away from them, trying to keep my gait graceful and smooth. All of this was perception, and the little things mattered.

First, I went to the bar and leaned over it, catching the eye of the bartender as I pushed my breasts out.

"What will it be?" he asked, his accent smooth and English.

"The strongest drink you've got." I pointed to the older man in the corner. "On him."

His gaze flicked back to the man, then he nodded as if it were totally normal for women to put drinks on the guy's tab.

Good. That was just the kind of guy who'd be susceptible to my charms. And if not my charms, then my suggestive magic.

I turned back to the bar in time to see the bartender push a tiny martini glass at me. The liquid within glowed a violent green.

Yeah, no way in hell I'd drink that, but it helped me play the part. Properly outfitted, I turned and headed to my target. I passed a potted plant and spilled about two thirds of my drink into it when no one was looking, then continued on.

As I approached the older man, I said a quick prayer to the fates that my friends would find that Acius hadn't yet been there. He could be here right now, but he didn't have much of a lead. Not if Cass could still feel the gem here.

The man watched me as I approached, his eyes lighting up at the sight of my chest. He almost drooled. It was so painfully obvious that I wanted to sigh.

But then, he probably thought I was here to sell him my favors. Didn't mean he had to be a sleaze about it, though.

I straightened my shoulders and gave him my iciest smile, then made sure to add some warmth to my eyes. I was good with this kind of thing—I'd used this sort of manipulation a lot in my earlier days. Make someone feel like they were the one to melt your icy heart and they'd be putty in your hands.

"You look like you need company," I purred.

"Why, little lady, I think I just might." He had a big, jovial voice. One that I might have liked—if only he hadn't called me *little lady.*

I swallowed bile and smiled, then slid onto the leather bench seat that made up his booth.

"What's a pretty girl like you doing in a place like this?"

My jaw nearly dropped at the bad line. I wanted to look down at my chest and say, "Don't you realize I'm a sure thing?"

On the other hand, I'd just been lamenting the fact that he was leering like a lech. Now he was trying his hand at flirting.

I forced a giggle, and it sounded rusty even to my own ears. He frowned slightly, and I forged onward. "Oh, I don't know. Just looking for a good time."

I batted my eyelashes.

He relaxed.

"Do you come here regularly?" he asked.

"First time." I shifted closer, getting a seriously pungent whiff of cologne. Whew. He could give Snakerton a run for his money.

I held my breath and sidled up even closer. I just needed to get within touching distance...

"Well, aren't you friendly." He grinned.

"You have no idea." I sliced my finger with my thumbnail. Pain welled, along with my blood, and I peeked out at the bar to see if anyone was looking.

No one was.

I turned back and swiped my finger over his forehead, quick as a snake.

I looked into his eyes, which flickered with confusion, and pushed my magic toward him, willing him to fall prey to my wiles. "Give me the information that I seek. Quickly. Quietly. Honestly."

A frown creased his brow, but just briefly. I pushed a bit more of my suggestive magic toward him, and he relaxed. "Of course. Anything for you, little lady."

"Don't call me little lady."

He nodded dumbly.

"I'm looking for a very valuable object that is under strong protection. The stone of destiny is somewhere in this city. I need to know where."

"There's only one place strong enough to protect a gem like that. The Academy of the Arcane Arts."

I smiled approvingly. "Have you seen the gem there?"

"No, I am a Councilor there, but I don't deal with the objects of power. But it's the only place in the city that would have something like that. The High Mages collect powerful objects for their collection. They protect them from the outside world."

This was a good place for it. "How do we get into the academy? I have to assume it is locked up tight."

"Oh, it is." He nodded eagerly, as if to please me by proving me right.

Please. I already knew I was right.

"How do we get in?" I prodded.

"Right. Right. Of course. You must enter via special carriage. That's how the academy knows you should be there. They have an arrangement with Sam McGee in town. Each carriage is run by its own special boiler. Only the best technology for Sam."

"Where is Sam?"

"He's at the west end of town, in the Machine District. The stables, specifically."

"Ahem." Someone cleared their throat at the other end of the table.

I nearly jumped. I'd been so into questioning this guy that I hadn't even noticed someone arrive.

I turned to the figure, a reedy man of about thirty who wore gold-rimmed spectacles and had the pinched expression of an accountant who'd spent too long looking over their books.

Or an assistant.

"What are you doing to Councilor Trevors?" The protectiveness in his tone indicated that I was right.

I was about to answer when I caught sight of the person who stood slightly behind him.

No, not a person.

A ghost.

She was slightly transparent, about five years younger than the assistant, and very pretty. Her dress was of the ornate variety favored by the women I'd seen so far, but her throat had been horribly slashed.

My eyes widened slightly, but I stifled a gasp.

"You can see me?" Her voice was sharp.

I squinted at her. I wanted to answer, but now wasn't the time.

I turned to the assistant and put on my iciest voice. "Just speaking to your boss. There is no need for you here. You're interrupting us."

"You're using magic on him." The man sent me an accusatory glare. "I can see the threads of it, going right from you to him."

Councilor Trevors harrumphed, sounding a bit like a put-out walrus.

"I've no idea what you're talking about," I lied. But shit, he could see my magic?

Damn, that was a handy power.

He definitely didn't buy my bluff. His brow scrunched up as he prepared to deliver another accusation.

The ghostly woman next to him stomped her foot. "Help me! I want to talk to him."

"Him?" I pointed to the assistant.

"Him." She nodded firmly. A golden locket at her throat glinted in the light. It was heart-shaped.

I pointed to it. "He in there?"

"He is."

Ah, bingo.

I looked at the assistant, who'd started rambling about prostitutes taking advantage.

"I'm going to slow you right down there." I held out my hands, palms forward, to get him to shut up and stop making a scene. Last thing I needed was to get dragged out of here. "My business with Councilor Trevors is none of *your* business. *However,* there's a lady ghost at your side who is very interested in talking to you."

He scoffed. "There isn't."

"She's wearing a golden locket with your picture inside. Heart-shaped."

His eyes widened. "No."

I looked at the girl. "What's your name?"

"Cora Bell."

"She's Cora Bell, and I think she was murdered."

His eyes filled with anguish. "I knew it. I knew she'd never leave me."

"She's never stopped following you." I looked at Cora, who nodded her agreement.

"I've just been trying to get him to listen! But he won't listen."

"Where is she?" The man spun, his eyes wild as he looked for her.

"What's going on?" Councilor Trevors asked.

Okay, there were too many cooks in this kitchen.

I turned to the councilor and re-nicked my finger, then swiped the blood over his forehead. "Sleep."

He slumped over, looking more unconscious than anything. Gingerly, I poked his chin until his head was propped against the back of the booth. This way, it was less obvious that he was passed out. Kind of.

"Where is she?" the assistant demanded.

I patted the bench. "Why don't you sit down, and we'll talk terms."

"Terms?" He scowled. "You want terms?"

"Of course I do. Do you think I was flirting with a man old enough to be my grandfather—who was basically drooling on my breasts, I might add—for fun?"

"Fair enough. The councilor should go for women his own age."

"You're telling me." I settled back against the seat as he joined me, then gestured for Cora to join us.

She floated over to the bench and sat next to the assistant.

"She's sitting next to you," I said.

"She is?" Stars basically filled his eyes at that.

"Yes. Now. Terms. I need to get into the academy of the Arcane Arts."

"You'll need Sam McGee."

"I know. I also need to know how to convince Sam McGee to take us. Sounds like he has a special contract with the academy, and he won't want to take just anyone in. I need to know his weak points." Odds were I could use my compelling magic, but just in case he was immune, I wanted to be prepared.

He nodded. "I can give you those. Give me Cora."

"I'll communicate for you. Not sure about actually *giving* her to you."

"Semantics."

"Works for me. Now tell me about Sam."

"Tell me about Cora first."

Stalemate. I held up my finger to get him to give me a second, then turned to Cora. "What do you want to tell him?"

"I want him to know where my body is. If he can find it, he can put my spirit into a machine, and I can live again."

"Wow, that's cool."

"What's cool?" the man demanded.

"Cora wants me to tell you where her body is."

He gasped, hope filling his eyes. No doubt he understood the rest of the deal with the machine, etc.

"I'll tell you that if you'll tell me about Sam."

The words spilled out of him so fast that it was almost hard to make them out. "If Sam resists doing what you want, tell him you'll take him to Lake Laberge. In the winter."

"Lake Laberge?"

"It's really cold. Sam hates being cold."

"That's it?"

"Oh, it will work." He sounded so confident that I didn't press him.

"All right, thanks." I looked at Cora. "Where's your body hidden?"

"Beneath the old mechanical oak in the widow's garden at the edge of town. She bound me with iron rope to keep my soul from leaving."

I winced. The widow sounded like a bitch.

I translated for the man, and anger flashed on his face. "I knew it was her."

"Well, go get her."

He nodded and stood, pushing his way through Cora's ephemeral form without realizing. He turned to me. "Tell her I love her."

Cora gasped.

"She can hear you."

"I love you, Cora."

My heart pinched a bit at the declaration, which was made to the wrong side of the table. Still, the sweetness was hard to ignore.

"Thank you." Cora turned to me, her expression intent. "Thank you so much."

"Sure." I'd have helped her no matter what, but it was nice that I'd gotten the bit of info about Sam McGee out of her man.

The assistant hurried off, with Cora following behind.

I woke the old walrus long enough to enchant him one last time and whispered, "Forget of me, I will of thee."

His eyes went cloudy, and he nodded.

I slid out of the booth and left, sweeping through the bar in my gown and looking for my friends. They were scattered around, each chatting up someone of the opposite sex. Bunch of hussies, my friends. But hey, it worked.

I headed for the exit, and Declan and Cass followed. Mari

nodded at me, and I nodded back. We convened near the exit, sticking to the shadows.

When Mari joined us a few minutes later, I asked, "Anything?"

"No one has seen him," Declan said.

Mari and Cass reported the same.

A bit of hope flared in my chest. Maybe Acius wasn't here yet. "Good. I've got a clue about where the gem is. We need to get a ride with Sam McGee, on the edge of town. He'll take us to where the gem is hidden."

"Nice work." Declan turned. "Let's get out of here."

We headed back out onto the street, which seemed to be even busier than it had been. More carriages rumbled through the streets and more people milled on the sidewalks. The cafes were full of patrons drinking from tiny silver cups.

A mechanical dog trotted by, barking in a tinny voice that clearly needed a little tweaking.

"This place is wild," Mari murmured as we cut through the streets.

"Seriously." I could spend hours here just looking at all the weird inventions in the shop windows.

Fortunately, the city was well marked. The Machine District wasn't hard to find, and we cut down the street, sticking close together. The crowd thinned out as we walked, replaced mostly with large buildings that clanged with noise from within.

"Whole place sounds like they're forging iron," Cass said.

"Probably are." I peered into a huge warehouse, spotting an enormous blimp that blinked with green lights. The basket beneath the balloon was built of wood and twisted copper. Pipes extended up to the balloon, which slowly filled.

Finally, we reached a large building marked with a sign that said The Stables. I pointed. "That's our man."

The four of us cut across the street and went to the main

door. Declan pushed it open and went first, his stance alert and ready for anything. I followed him into a massive stable that was stocked full of horseless carriages. Though they looked like regular old-fashioned carriages, each one was outfitted with a big metal box strapped to the back. Tubes and dials decorated the box.

Must be the special boiler that the assistant had spoken of.

"Hello?" I called.

My voice echoed in the huge space.

A rustling sounded from the back, and a man eventually appeared, his apron dirty with grease and his face stained with soot. Beneath the black smudges, his skin had a distinctly blue cast. Like he'd been frozen, or something. He approached with a stiff gait, moving a bit slower than the average person.

"Don't have any trips planned for today." Confusion creased his face.

"We need to go to the Academy of the Arcane Arts," I said. "Now."

He laughed. "I definitely don't have a trip planned there." He tapped his head. "I think I'd know about that."

"We need to go immediately, and you'll help us."

He scoffed. "Or what?"

"Or we'll take you to Lake Laberge." I drew a transport charm out of my pocket, which was actually a strange effect, considering that I had to reach through the illusion of my dress to get to the pants pocket beneath. "I'll chuck this transport charm on the ground, we'll grab you, and shove you through."

He whitened. "You wouldn't."

"I hear it's cold there this time of year."

He shivered.

Maybe he had been frozen?

"Come on, friend," Declan said. "Just help us out. We're

doing this to save a lot of people." Quickly, he explained what we were working against. Who was at risk.

Sam frowned, clearly swayed but not entirely convinced.

"And if you don't help us," Mari said. "Someone even worse is coming."

"We'll return the stone once we know it's safe to do so," Cass said. "Namely, when the *someone worse* is dead."

"I don't know..." Sam said.

"Don't think about it so hard," I said. "Just think about Lake Laberge."

He winced. I knew I was going for the gut, but we didn't have time to spare.

"Fine." He scowled. "I'll do it. But only because it will help a lot of people."

"Thank you."

He gestured for us to follow. "Come on with me. I've got just the carriage." He turned to look at me as we walked back. "If you're intent on sneaking in, you'd better be crafty about it. I don't want you getting caught. It'll come back on me."

"All the more reason for you to tell us everything you know about the place," Declan said.

Sam harrumphed, but clearly he agreed. As we walked through his enormous warehouse full of carriages, he described a bit of the layout, and explained how we'd enter via a side entrance, riding in a totally enclosed carriage. If pressed, he'd explain that we were vampires with a particularly strong aversion to sun.

It didn't take long to get one of the carriages up and running, and we all piled in. I sat next to Sam in the front, watching as he manipulated a dozen different dials and levers.

The boiler on the back rumbled to life, and the carriage began to vibrate. It pulled forward, a rickety ride that bounced over the cobblestones below. We pulled out onto the main street.

The sun was beginning to set, and the gas lamps provided most of the light that gleamed golden on the street.

"Why do you hate Lake Laberge so much?" I asked as he navigated us through the town. "Is it really that cold?"

"Look at me. I'm frozen solid." He knocked on one arm with his fist, and it did look pretty hard. "I went over there for the gold and came back different. Frozen."

"Wow. I didn't even know that was possible."

"Lucky to have come back at all. Not that I could go home." He met my gaze. "People would notice I'm different. But not here. Here, I'm just as normal as anyone else."

"But are you cold all the time?"

"All the time." He sounded bitter about it, too.

Couldn't blame him. "If I get out of this alive, and I manage to save my town, come visit me in Magic's Bend. I'll see if I can make something to help you."

"Yeah?" He gave me an appreciative look.

"Yeah. No promises, but I bet I can whip up something."

"I'll hold you to it."

Wally appeared next to me, his dark fur wafting and his red eyes bright. He wore a little leather vest covered in metal toggles.

"Hey, Wally," I said.

Sam's eyes brightened on the cat. "Hellcat! Give me a blast."

Wally looked at him, head tilted as he thought about it. Then he blasted his flame on Sam, who sighed with delight but didn't melt.

Through the flames, Sam gave me a look. "On particularly bad days, I climb right inside one of these boilers."

Ouch.

"Nearly there."

Thank fates. I was running out of small talk for Sam.

He pointed ahead. "There it is."

The massive building appeared at the end of the street. We

actually weren't far from where we'd entered the city—probably only a couple of blocks.

The academy itself was built entirely of dark red brick, with hundreds of windows across its four-story front. A cupola tower protruded off the top of the building, and the whole place looked like the enchanted academy that it no doubt was. Gas lamps flickered at even intervals along the iron gate that surrounded the property.

"Welcome to the Academy of the Arcane Arts," Sam said. "The most deadly place in town."

12

Sam drove the carriage right up to the massive wrought iron gate. Flourishing curlicues of metal were intertwined with iron flowers, but somehow, the whole thing looked menacing instead of inviting. A guard stood behind the gate, his heavy brow creased as he inspected the carriage.

Sam waved.

I held my breath.

Finally, the guard nodded and pulled open the gate. It creaked, groaning ominously as he pulled it all the way open and swept his arm out, gesturing for us to enter.

Sam pulled the carriage through without looking at the guard, then took a right and drove around to the side of the building. I leaned over and looked out the window, studying the academy as we passed. Figures flickered behind the windows, but it was impossible to make out any detail.

"You're entering via the staff entrance," he said. "There are fewer people there, and less security as well. But remember—if you are caught, lie."

"Lie. Got it. And if we want to get out of here, how do we do it?"

"Out of the academy or out of Steamtown?"

"Steamtown."

"The only way to exit is via the same door you entered. You must go back to the oil rig."

"Crap."

"It's only two blocks away, down the street leading away from the front of the academy."

As I'd thought earlier, thank fates. Hopefully we wouldn't have to run for it, but with our luck...

Sam drove us around to the side and stopped the carriage under a huge stone portico. We got out, and I looked back at him.

"Remember to come visit," I said.

"Can I keep your cat?"

"No."

No, Wally said at the same time.

"Then I'll visit." He saluted us goodbye, then pulled around to the side.

"Any clues?" I asked Cass.

"My dragon sense is pulling us inside, but other than that, no."

"Then let's follow," Declan said.

Cass led the way through the side entrance. The hall was wide and paved with smooth gray stone. Ornate carved wood decorated the bottom half of the walls, while the top half was done in a floral velvet wallpaper. Gas lamps flickered golden against the wall, creating an inviting old-world atmosphere.

Except for the wooziness that struck as soon as we stepped inside.

"Whoa." I pressed a hand to my head. "Feel that?"

"Some kind of spell?" Declan asked.

"I think so," Mari said.

"I think the building knows we're not supposed to be here." I squinted, trying to make the hallway come into focus. Which way were we supposed to go?

It looked like there were dozens of hallways leading off this space, but it hadn't looked like this when we'd first walked in, right before the spell had hit us.

The sound of voices filtered down the hall, followed by the clicking of heeled shoes on the stone.

"Shhhh," I whispered. "Someone is coming."

"I'll make us invisible," Cass said. "Just stand really still, pressed up against a wall."

I moved toward the wall, my steps as wobbly as a drunk's. What the hell was this spell?

Everyone around me disappeared, and I pressed my back against the wall, holding my breath. The sound of voices grew louder, and four people turned a corner.

There were two women and two men. Each one was dressed in long black robes, though the women's robes had a bit of dark lace trim at the bottom.

Tension crackled on the air as they approached, absorbed in a conversation that included phrases like "water to steam ratio" and "light refraction quotient."

Whatever they were talking about, it was above my pay grade. One of the women stopped, her nose wrinkling. "Do you smell that?"

A man with sleek blond hair halted next to her, sniffing the air. "Smells like a bar. Liquor and smoke."

Ah, the Steam and Whistle, where we'd just been.

"The students." The dark-haired woman shook her head. "Always out partying."

"They'll learn." The man tsked. "They always do."

Come on. Pass us by.

We didn't need to start a fight right now, and I wasn't keen on going against a bunch of professors.

The four of them kept moving, walking past us with only a few inches to spare between my chest and the shoulder of the dark-haired woman.

They disappeared into a room farther down the hall, and my shoulders slumped with relief. Thank fates.

Except the hallway was still hazy and my balance still wobbly.

"Can anyone see straight?" Mari asked.

"No," Cass said. "And there are about a hundred hallways leading off of this one. That's not even possible."

I blinked, trying to clear my vision. This was such a benign spell, but so effective. The building was guarding itself. If we didn't find a way around this, we'd stumble around like drunken morons until someone caught us.

I drew in a slow breath and pressed my hand flat against the wall. I could just barely feel the charm that imbued the wood and wallpaper. It was a tricky one, but it seeped slowly from the surface, leaching out into the air that we breathed.

I fed my nullification magic into the wall, trying to repress the magic that fueled the spell. It pushed back, burning my hand.

"Ouch!" I hissed, yanking my hand back. "This spell bites back."

"Try harder," Mari whispered.

I snorted at her, then did as she commanded, pressing my hand to the wall and forcing my nullification magic into the surface. I hit it with a surge of power, working as fast and hard as I could.

"I can see straight!" Cass said.

"Same," Declan said.

"Whew." I blinked as my vision cleared and the wooziness faded. "Let's get moving. I don't know how long I can keep this up."

I dragged my hand along the wall as we walked, forcing my magic into the surface to keep the spell repressed. I could feel it fighting me.

I looked back at Cass. "Which way?"

"Ahead, I think." She frowned. "Maybe a bit to the left. If I hear someone coming, I'll make us invisible."

She led us through a warren of twisting hallways and rooms. Finally, we were far enough away from the entry that I tested removing my hand. The disorientation didn't return, thank fates.

"I think we're getting closer," Cass said. "I can feel it tugging on me. Come this way."

She led us into a huge room that was filled with clouds of amorphous, colorful gases. The lights hanging from the high ceiling were dimmed, but the gases glowed with their own colorful light. They floated in front of the walls to the sides of us, all different shades of the rainbow.

"This is strange." Mari eyed the gases warily.

"I guess this is what they mean by arcane arts?" I shivered as I passed in front of a dark blue gas. The cloud was about as tall as me and a few feet wide. It pulsed with emotion.

"It feels like grief," Declan said.

We walked in front of a cloud of red gas. Rage pulsed deep in my chest, memories of Acius rising to the surface. Memories of Aunt. Uncle. Anger simmered deep inside, threatening to explode within me. I gritted my teeth.

"Anyone else pissed off?" Cass asked. "Because I've got some pretty powerful rage right now."

"It's got to be the red gas." Declan's voice was rough with anger. He picked up the pace, moving fast to get away from the cloud's influence.

I quickened my step, grateful when the rage subsided. I had plenty of that of my own, thanks. No need for it to be enhanced by a weird science experiment.

We were nearly to the end of the room when one of the gas clouds moved. It drifted from the wall, floating toward us quickly. It encapsulated Mari in seconds. A wail burst from her throat, and she collapsed.

Shit.

I lunged for her, my hand getting caught in the mist as I grabbed for her arm. Every bad memory I'd ever had surged to the front of my mind. All the loss and sadness. It nearly crippled me. I gasped, unwilling to let go of Mari's arm but unable to move.

From the corner of my eye, I saw Declan freeze. The gas had surrounded him. Agony twisted his features, grief and pain at memories better forgotten.

Somehow, the power of the gas was so strong that we couldn't even move. I strained, pulling at Mari, but I couldn't shift so much as an inch. Every muscle ached, but I was stuck. We'd be frozen here until someone rescued us.

If they ever did. What was the punishment for breaking into a place like this?

From the corner of my eye, I spotted Cass. The gas hadn't gotten to her yet.

"I've got this," she muttered, holding out her hands, palms facing forward. A blast of wind shot from her hands, blowing the gas away. Immediately, the memories faded, taking with it the grief and pain.

I straightened, tugging on Mari to help her stand. She staggered upright.

"Shit, sorry. I was too loud." Her wide eyes met mine. "Let's get the hell out of here."

Together we raced from the room, passing more colorful clouds that emitted emotions that ranged from joy to ennui to terror and everything in between. Cass kept up the blasts of wind, making a path for us toward the exit.

We spilled out into another corridor, then passed through a room that was totally full of tubes of bubbling, colorful liquid. The glass piping extended across the ceiling, hundreds of pathways filled with colorful solutions.

"Shit, don't break anything," Cass said.

We made it out safely, into an enormous square foyer that extended four stories up. A dozen open air staircases were pressed against the walls, leading to higher rooms.

Immediately, the ground fell out from beneath me as the room twisted. I slammed into a set of stairs, which were now underneath me, at least as far as gravity was concerned.

"Shit!" Mari hissed, scrambling on the stairs as the room continued to move around us. It was like trying to survive inside an MC Escher painting.

We struggled not to fall too far, and I shot Cass a desperate glance. "Can you tell which way we need to go?"

Her forehead screwed up in concentration, and she pointed to a doorway on the second level. It was directly across from us. "There."

The room was twisting so that the doorway would be below us soon. We could jump into it, but aiming would be a problem. Declan launched himself into the air, his wings flaring wide.

As the room twisted, I clung tight to the stair railing. Cass and Mari held on next to me, their faces strained. Gravity pulled harder as the room rotated around us, flipping us nearly upside down. Declan positioned himself below us, right between our exit and where we hung on to the railings.

"Jump and I'll toss you in the right direction," he said.

Oh fates, this was insane. "I'll test it."

I let go of the railing, falling fast and hard. Declan grabbed my arm and adjusted my trajectory, swinging me slightly left and letting go. I fell the last twenty feet, plunging right through the open door and sliding onto a stone floor.

Gasping, I scrambled upright. My head was still spinning, but the room itself wasn't. I hurried to the door that led into the crazy room, looking up to see my friends dangling above me, still clutching the railing.

"Jump! It's safe!"

Mari let go, and Declan grabbed her in midair, tossing her toward the doorway where I stood. She fell toward me, and I darted out of the way, grabbing her arm and helping her land.

Cass came flying in a half second later, followed by Declan. Everyone staggered to their feet, and we circled up.

"This place is a hell of a trip," Declan said.

"No kidding." I turned in a circle.

"I feel it." Mari's eyes widened. "We're close."

Hell yeah. Mari had a bit of seeker sense. Not nearly as strong as Cass's dragon sense, but still very handy.

"Lead the way." I gestured for her to go ahead.

She led us out through the door and into another hall.

Footsteps sounded in the distance, and Cass whispered, "Invisibility coming your way."

Two people turned into our hallway. They walked close together, whispering about something. Fancy glasses adorned each face, the rims decorated with gears and toggles. Obviously they were meant to do something, but I had no idea what.

As they neared, they looked up. Their eyes widened when they saw us, and they stiffened.

Oh shit.

That's what the fancy glasses could do.

I whispered, "They see us."

Mari lunged for the one nearest her—a tall woman with a beak-like nose and an aura of power that made me shiver. Cass, who was closest to Mari, leapt for them both, slapping her hand over the woman's mouth so she couldn't shout.

The man who stood five feet in front of me was a thin, wiry

fellow who looked like he'd just woken up from an eight-year nap. His owlish eyes widened even more when they landed on me as I approached. "Intruders!"

I darted for him, then smacked my hand over his mouth and got him in a headlock. Magic surged from him, an electric pulse that tore through my muscles.

I yelped and dropped him, and he scrambled back, raising his hands.

Declan lunged for him, grabbing the man by the arm.

I straightened and sliced my finger with my thumbnail, then swiped the blood across the man's forehead and whispered, "Sleep."

He slumped, dangling from Declan's grip.

Next to me, Cass had knocked the woman unconscious, and Mari was busy binding her arms and mouth. Both Cass and Mari had frizzy hair.

"Was she electric too?" I asked.

They nodded.

"This gig is harder when you can't kill them, that's for sure," Cass said.

I grinned. True, it was easier to hurl a dagger, but we couldn't go around murdering professors, no matter how dangerous they were.

Declan swept the unconscious man up in his arms, looking around. "Anyone see a handy closet?"

Mari pointed to a small door a few feet down. "That might work."

It did turn out to be a closet, so we stashed the unconscious people in there. Declan and I rifled through their pockets, each pulling free a key ring studded with old-fashioned skeleton keys. Finished, we shut the door, hiding the evidence of our crimes.

"There." I dusted off my hands. "Out of sight. Out of mind."

"We're close," Cass said.

"There." Mari pointed to a door at the end of the hall. "It's in there."

"And still no sign of Acius," Declan said.

Hell yeah. We might just beat him to it. The sneaky bastard had shown up at the last second last time, but unless he blasted his way through the back wall of this building, we had a lead on him.

"Let's go beat this bastard." Mari's brow set, and she strode toward the door.

We followed, moving quickly to avoid running into anyone else.

We reached the door, which was massively heavy. The four of us stood in front of it, inspecting it for any magical charms that might protect it.

"There's just the big lock." Mari pointed to the complicated metal device. "No other charms that I can feel."

"Ditto," I said.

Declan and Cass confirmed the same.

I tugged the key ring that I'd taken from the woman out of my pocket and found the biggest key. It slid smoothly into the lock, but wouldn't turn. I tried again, not wanting to twist too hard for fear of breaking it, but it wouldn't go.

"What's wrong?" Mari asked.

"Won't turn."

Declan bent and looked at the key in my hand, his brow creasing. "I'm going to try something. Hang on."

He rose and sprinted off down the hall, returning to the closet where we'd stashed the professors. He retrieved the still unconscious body of the woman and carried her back to us.

He met my eye. "Leave the key stuck in the lock, but step back."

I did as he asked, and he moved into position in front of the lock, still holding the woman.

"Just going to try this one little thing." He grunted as he maneuvered her body so he could wrap her hand around the base of the key. He held her hand in his, then twisted the lock.

It turned smoothly, and the lock snicked as the mechanism unhooked. Declan moved the woman's hand from the lock to the door handle, then pulled it open with her touch.

He glanced at me. "Can you hold it open while I return her to the closet?"

I grabbed the door, and while he ran her back, I slowly pulled it open, peering inside. My jaw dropped. "Well, shit."

"What is it?" Mari jostled into position, peering into the enormous room.

In half a second, we took in the whole crazy space.

It was easily four stories tall, windowless and dark except for the glowing pipes of water that stuck right into a huge waterfall that poured from the far wall. They stuck into the top of the water column, then rose to the ceiling and zigzagged across the top, heading toward the walls and disappearing inside, going toward other places in the building.

The waterfall itself was at least thirty feet across and thirty feet high, a solid wall of pounding seawater—I could smell the salt from where I stood—that poured into a pit in the ground, disappearing from the room entirely.

It seemed to be generating power to all of the other contraptions that were hooked up to it. Little water wheels and other metal bits and bobs were stuck up to the middle of the waterfall, generating hydro energy as they whirred and buzzed.

Standing at the base of the falls were eight guards, each of them tall and broad, wearing identical steel gray uniforms covered in bits of metal that looked like they were somehow protective, but I couldn't figure out how.

Their gazes riveted to us, and they raised their hands, which flamed with different colors of magic.

"Shit." Mari echoed my statement, and it was the only pause we had.

I raced into the room, my sister at my side. Cass and Declan followed. I drew a dagger from the ether, determined to wound instead of kill. I *so* preferred fighting demons. Much easier.

I sprinted toward the guards on the left. Declan launched himself into the air, and Cass raced for the ones on the right.

Mari ran toward the corner of the room, drawing her bow and arrows from the ether as she went. She set up shop behind one of the huge tables that was covered with weird equipment, then carefully aimed at a guard and sent an arrow flying. It nailed him in the leg just as he released a massive fireball at me.

He fell, screaming, and I dodged right, barely avoiding the blast. It streaked past, flaming with heat that singed my hair.

I hurled my dagger at another man's thigh. The metal plunged into the muscle, and he howled, dropping to the ground. The sound was absorbed by the roar of the waterfall, thank fates.

Declan plunged down toward a guard in the middle, his huge wings carrying him fast. The guard looked up at him, raising a hand that glowed with green magic. Acid?

He hurled the blast of emerald light at Declan, who dodged. The light turned to liquid in midair, splashing Declan on the side of the thigh as he neared the guard. Declan winced, pain streaking across his face, but didn't slow his approach. He landed in front of the guard, moving so fast it was hard to make out his motions. One second he was in the air; the next, the guard was unconscious at his feet, victim to a hard hit to the head that would definitely give him a concussion.

As I sprinted for a guard, I kept tabs on Declan and Cass out of the corner of my eye.

Declan whirled and lunged for another guard, while a fifth hurled a blast of blue magic at Cass—a sonic boom, probably.

The red-headed FireSoul had a black glass dagger gripped in each hand. She darted left, taking a hit to the shoulder. That arm went limp, but she managed to keep a grip on the dagger. She hurled the blade from her good arm, hitting a guard in the leg, then grabbed the second knife from her now-injured hand, throwing it at a third guard. It nailed him in the shoulder, and he wailed, spinning backward and slamming into the wall.

Mari hit a seventh guard with an arrow, right in the shoulder. "I've got the eighth," she shouted at my back. "Put them to sleep!"

I diverted my plan—which had been to take out the final guard—and sprinted to one who was yanking a dagger from his thigh and struggling to rise.

He shot a blast of fire at me from his slumped position, and I dived left. It slammed into the side of my shin, and I winced. Heat seared. I rolled on the ground, dousing the flames as pain surged through me.

When the blaze was out, I rose and ran toward him, slicing my fingertip with my thumbnail and letting the blood rise. He struggled upward, clearly trying to rebuild the firepower within him to send another blast at me. Stronger mages need less time to recoup their magic, and this guy would be good to go in seconds.

When I neared him, I pulled the same trick that I'd used on Acius. I raised my hand to my mouth and blew across my palm like I was blowing him a kiss.

Pale white smoke drifted off my palm, and I whispered, "Sleep. Weaken."

The smoke drifted over the guard, and he weakened, slumping to the side and going limp. I turned to the other guard, who was stifling the blood that flowed from his shoulder, and put him to sleep as well.

I turned to make sure that all the guards were unconscious.

They were, no doubt due to Declan's quick fist. He and Cass were staring around the room, frowns on their faces.

Mari appeared at my side, then bent to inspect the wounds. "Just want to make sure no one bleeds out."

"Smart." I left her to the task and paced around the room, trying to figure out where the hell the gem could be. This looked more like a power generation room than a place that was meant to guard valuable objects.

Cass approached. "I think it's behind the falls. I can feel a tug from there, and that's where the guards were positioned."

Shit.

I turned toward the waterfall. It thundered down with tremendous force, plunging straight into the crevasse below. "If we try to jump it, the water pressure will force us into the crevasse."

And that would *definitely* kill us.

13

“There’s got to be a way to stop it.” Declan launched himself into the air, flying up toward the top of the falls.

I spun in a circle, looking around the rest of the room for levers or buttons or anything that might be a command station to control the falls.

“It’s manual!” Declan shouted from above. He pointed to two heavy levers on either side of the flowing water. “We need to push those at the same time, and the water will shut off.”

I eyed them. “I can do one if you’ll do the other.”

Declan landed next to the lever on the right.

I strode to the left, looking at Mari and Cass. “Get ready.”

They lined up in front of the falls as I gripped the lever.

“On my count,” Declan said.

I waited, and he counted down. On one, I began to push. The lever resisted.

Shit, it was difficult, even with my unnatural strength.

I glanced over at Declan. His lever was beginning to move. Corded muscles strained at his shirt, and his brow creased with effort, but he was moving the lever. I leaned into mine, pushing harder. It budged, but barely.

"Mari!" I shouted. She had the same unnatural strength that I did, and we were going to need it.

She loped over, then bent low, getting a grip on the lower part of the lever's shaft. We both pushed, grunting and sweating, and the lever began to move, creaking downward.

"It's working!" Cass shouted.

The waterfall began to slow, as if it were being cut off behind the wall. As I pushed, I wondered if we would find Acius behind the water, waiting with the gem clutched in his hands and an evil smile on his face. I shook away the thought.

No.

We'd beat him. We had to.

My muscles ached and burned, but finally, the water ceased entirely. Cass sprinted forward and leapt over the crevasse.

"Go," I grunted to Mari.

She nodded, then let go of the lever and sprinted. I leaned heavily into the iron post, keeping my weight on it, but it was exponentially more difficult without her.

I glanced over at Declan and met his eyes.

"On my count," he said.

When he reached one, I let go of the lever and sprinted toward the crevasse in the ground. Declan raced alongside me. From above, I could hear the creaking and groaning of the mechanism that held the water in place. It was starting to release.

I pushed myself faster, running as hard as I could. As I reached the crevasse, water began to pour from the ceiling. I leapt, soaring across the gaping black hole beneath me. Droplets of water rained onto my head. I landed hard on the other side, just as the water crashed down behind me. Declan made it just in time.

Heart thundering, I stared at the monstrosity ahead of me,

shock coursing through me. It wasn't Acius. Oh no, he was nowhere to be seen.

Instead, a massive mechanical octopus sat in front of us, right in the middle of a huge, domed room. The creature was at least forty feet tall, with arms of steel plates and gears beneath the legs. A green gem was clutched in its mouth.

The gears beneath the legs began to turn, metal creaking and groaning. The legs shifted, huge metal appendages that could smack me right into the wall, probably hard enough that I turned into a pancake.

Wally appeared next to me. *This is cool.*

"That's one word for it." I looked at Mari. "Let's try lightning first."

She nodded. "Step back, guys."

Cass and Declan did as we asked, and Mari and I sliced our palms. As the blood welled, we positioned ourselves on either side of the octopus. I called upon the lightning within me, letting it flow to the surface. It crackled and burned.

I met Mari's gaze, and we released the energy. The lightning bolt cracked into existence, streaking between our palms as a bright white bolt. It struck the octopus hard, and the machine shuddered.

Then the lightning bounced off, headed straight back for us. I lunged left, skidding hard on the rock as the current nearly slammed into me. It plowed into the stone wall, breaking off chunks of rock.

Aching, I stumbled to my feet. "Shit, that's some strong reflective magic."

The current had clearly triggered something in the machine, which was winding up, legs starting to undulate as metal creaked and groaned.

"Looks like we're doing this the hard way." Mari met my gaze. "Could I have a mace?"

"Anytime." I called on my mace from the ether, then handed it over to Mari.

She grinned and took it. "Thanks."

I drew another one for myself and looked at Declan. "Go for the gem. We'll take care of the legs."

They were moving faster now, undulating like waves.

Declan launched himself into the air, wings flaring wide.

Cass conjured an enormous fireball, hurling it at one of the legs. The limb shuddered and jerked, but didn't break off. She hurled another. She'd get it—she just needed enough time.

Wally raced for one of the undulating arms, leaping toward it and slamming into it with his feet. The arm shuddered but didn't break. The little cat bounced off and tried again, hitting it harder this time.

I sprinted for the beast, swinging my mace. I arced it high, slamming it into one of the legs as another one tried to smash down onto me. Metal shattered above my head as my iron ball crashed into the octopus. I dived left, dragging the mace with me as the second leg nearly crushed me.

In the air, Declan dodged the legs that slapped at him. They were as fast as he was, which meant he did more dodging than approaching.

To my right, Mari took out a leg with her mace, while Cass blasted them with fireballs. All around, metal groaned and creaked. I dodged the limbs as fast as I could, but they were so quick. One caught me in the stomach. Instinctively, I dropped my mace and grabbed onto the limb, clinging hard so it couldn't throw me against the wall. My heart thundered.

When it raised me up and tried to shake me off, I dropped and landed in a crouch, lunging for my mace. I swept it up and swung, darting aside as I got up the momentum to slam it into the octopus's limb.

The metal shuddered and slowed as I damaged the gears beneath the metal plating.

"Almost there!" Mari shouted.

There were only three limbs left, just few enough that Declan was able to dart in and grab the gem from the mouth.

Immediately, a siren began to wail.

Shit.

A limb came flying at him. He saw it just in time and caught my eye, shouting, "Catch!"

He tossed the gem to me right before an arm slammed into him, sending him flying through the air. I snagged it and gripped it tight, then raced for Declan, who lay crumpled on the ground. Cass and Mari darted out of the way of the remaining arms.

I reached Declan and knelt by his side, then gripped his shoulder and shook. "Come on!"

He groaned and opened his eyes.

Worry twisted my insides. "Are you okay?"

"Yeah." He groaned and stood. "Just a little broken."

"Can you run?" The siren wailed. "Because we really need to run."

"Yeah." He grunted, and I helped him up, then we sprinted for the exit.

"Come on!" Mari shouted. She stood near the falls, her hand hovering over a big red button.

We sprinted for her, and she slammed her hand onto it. The waterfall ceased flowing, and the four of us leapt over the crevasse. Almost immediately, the water began pouring again.

There was no one in the power generation room—yet.

"We just have to get to a window," Cass said. "Thank fates we're on the first floor."

We raced from the room, Declan limping but moving fast. The hall outside was empty, and we headed for the nearest window. Wally sprinted ahead of us, leaping up when he reached the window and blasting a huge ball of flame at it. The glass shattered, and he soared through.

We leapt out after him and landed right at the edge of the lawn.

Cass pointed to a huge oak tree next to the cast iron fence. "I'll make us invisible. Jump the fence near the oak tree, then I'll make us visible again and we'll run for the exit to this world."

The downside of Cass's illusion power was that we couldn't see each other, either, so it was necessary to occasionally regain visibility to make sure we hadn't lost one another.

We disappeared a half second later, but I kept a tight grip on Declan's hand. I didn't know how badly he was injured, and if he fell behind, I wouldn't see him.

Together, we sprinted for the oak tree. My lungs burned as we ran.

I glanced back, spotting people running past the windows, no doubt headed to the octopus room. Our invisibility bought us some time, but probably not much.

We reached the tree, and I let go of Declan's hand to climb over. I landed hard on the other side. A moment later, I became visible again, along with the others.

"We're only two blocks from the gate." Declan's face was pinched with pain as he pointed down the road.

"Invisibility coming at you," Cass said.

I grabbed Declan's hand right before we disappeared, and we sprinted down the street, dodging people as best we could. It was some kind of rush hour, though, and the sidewalks were packed with people in fancy outfits. We slammed into them, pushing them aside.

They shouted and stumbled, confusion flashing across their faces when they realized they couldn't see their attackers.

When I glanced back, I spotted mechanical flying machines

in the air. They shot off the roof of the academy, spreading out quickly. They were too small to hold people, but I'd bet a hundred bucks they were enchanted to search for us.

"Almost there," Declan said from beside me.

My heartbeat thundered as we ran, and I kept glancing up at the machines that hunted us. Soon, they'd notice that something was weird on this street, what with all the people falling everywhere as we bowled into them.

Up ahead, I spotted the massive iron door that would lead out of this realm.

"Slow up!" I shouted.

We needed to sneak up to the gate—or at least, not cause chaos as we approached. I slowed, careful not to bump into anyone, and finally skidded to a halt in front of the massive iron door.

I gripped the stone tight, sweat dripping down my back.

The four of us appeared as Cass dropped the invisibility spell. We stared at the huge door in horror. It was decorated with just as many gears as it had been on the other side, though they weren't as rusty.

Exiting required solving another puzzle, just like the last one. Except this one had no smooth, grooved lines showing which direction to move the dials. They all had to touch, but one had to know *how.*

There were no clues at all.

I looked at all my friends, spotting equal looks of confusion.

No one had any idea.

And everyone was starting to look at us funny. Above, the flying machines began to circle.

We were screwed.

"I thought you'd be here ten minutes ago!" An annoyed voice sounded from my left.

I turned, spotting the assistant from earlier. He nodded at me and winked. My mind raced, temporarily confused.

Oh... We were supposed to play along.

"I'm sorry we're so late." I searched for the ghost, but didn't see her. Maybe he'd already saved her?

My heart thundered in my ears as I looked from him to the flying machines.

Shit, shit, shit.

"Come, come, let's get this door open." He strode toward it and began fiddling with the gears, moving them in a pattern that seemed to come easily to him. As he worked, he looked back over his shoulder and whispered, "Thank you for the help with Cora. I've found her."

"You're welcome." I pointed to the door. "Thanks for this."

"I had a feeling you wouldn't be able to manage it, and after what you did for me, I wanted to help. When I heard the siren go off and saw the drones, I knew you'd need it."

"Thank you. Seriously." Anxiety thrummed through me as I checked out the drones again. "Hurry, please."

"And...done!" He stepped back. The door creaked upward, rising like a garage. "You must walk through this time."

I didn't need telling twice, and neither did my friends.

Thank fates, we'd made it.

The four of us rushed through, arriving on the blustery platform of the oil rig in the middle of the North Sea.

Right into chaos.

Demons crowded the platform, at least two dozen of them. Hulking and enormous, they'd clearly been lying in wait for us. Acius stood behind them, an evil smile on his face.

My stomach jumped into my throat.

That bastard.

He'd never even tried to get into the Academy of the Arcane

Arts. Maybe he couldn't, or he'd always planned to try to ambush us.

Cass hurled a transport charm to the ground. It didn't even explode. No poof of silver dust burst upward.

Shit.

"We can't transport." Cass gestured to the electric circle surrounding the platform. "It's gotta be the barrier that's preventing it."

I had no idea what kind of magic it was, but it belonged to Acius somehow. The demons prowled closer.

"I'm calling Nielson," Cass said as she raised a hand that burned with flame. "We just have to hold them off for a bit, and she'll have us right out of here."

"Hurry." Mari drew her bow and arrow from the ether. It wouldn't work for long—the demons would be too close soon—but she was fast with it.

"Not yet," I murmured out of the corner of my mouth. "If we can hold him off with chatting, maybe we won't get bloody."

Or dead.

Mari nodded almost imperceptibly.

Acius cackled and stepped forward.

My blood ran cold, despite the fact that I now had protection against his potions.

"How I've been looking forward to your arrival!" he shouted, his gaze right on me.

He'd be coming for me, no matter what. I swallowed hard.

As surreptitiously as I could, I passed the gemstone to Declan. "Fly it out of here if you have to."

"I'm not leaving you."

"I'm fine." I imbued it with as much determination as I could, and gave him a hard look. "And there's more at stake than just me."

He scowled at me, but I knew he agreed. And I *could* handle myself. Even against Acius.

"She's close," Cass murmured.

"You're a coward, Acius!" I shouted. "Waiting for us, crouching like a hyena to pick at scraps."

His brow lowered and his mouth flattened. He raised a hand, then shouted a command in a language I didn't recognize.

The demons charged.

"Shit. I went too far." I looked at Mari. "Time for the bow."

"No kidding." She fired, arrow after arrow, faster than any normal person could ever hope to.

Cass raised her hand, which glowed with flame. "There's no actual oil on this rig, right?"

"Haven't seen any." I drew my mace and began to swing it. "I think it's just for show."

"Good." Cass hurled a fireball at the nearest demon and nailed him right in the head.

He howled and stumbled backward, smacking at the flames that were quickly devouring his face.

Mari and Cass took care of the long-range attack, while I charged right into the fray, Declan at my side. He wielded his sword, and I swung my mace.

"Get out of here if it looks too dicey!" I shouted as I slammed my mace into the skull of the nearest demon. He was tall, with pale green skin and long, curled horns. He hissed, spitting acid, and I dodged, barely avoiding a sizzling, disgusting mess.

Declan plunged his sword into the gut of a stocky red demon while shooting another with lightning from his free hand. "I will."

The demon to my right—a smoke demon, from the look of him—swiped out with his huge claws. I lunged right, avoiding the blow, and he followed it up with a smoke blast.

I ducked at the last second, feeling the rush of air over my head as it soared past me. I charged him, smashing the mace into his head. He made no sound, if you disregarded the crunch of his skull as he collapsed.

Acius seemed content to hang out at the back. Which was fucking weird. And scary.

"Why isn't he attacking?" I asked Declan, who fought nearby, never leaving my side.

His lightning struck repeatedly, and the steel of his sword flashed. "No idea, but it can't be good."

My breath heaved and sweat poured down my face as I fought. The demons seemed to appear from nowhere, more and more of them. Soon, I had to switch out for my sword. They were getting too close—and too many—for the mace.

Behind me, I caught sight of Mari and Cass. They'd switched to short-range weapons as well, both wielding swords with ferocity.

"Nielson?" I shouted.

"Soon!" Cass hacked at the neck of a demon who was about her height but twice as wide, then ducked a fireball shot by another.

Within two minutes, we were overrun. There was no hope of defeating them all. No matter how fast I swung my blade, I couldn't get them all. In the distance, Acius was smiling.

Bastard.

"Get out of here," I grunted at Declan. "Too late."

"No." He swung his blade so hard it chopped an enormous demon right in half. The torso fell off and splatted to the ground. With his other hand, he shot a blast of lightning at an oncoming blue demon.

The lightning lit him up, and he dropped like a stone. Declan hit another with the same attack.

"You can attack from the air, then." I grunted as I plunged

my sword into the gut of a nearby attacker. "Just get that gem out of here."

Four more demons appeared out of thin air.

My heart rate spiked, and sweat chilled my skin.

How the hell was Acius doing this?

Every muscle in my body ached, and my hands were so slippery with sweat and blood that it was hard to maintain a grip on my sword.

"Go, or it's all for nothing!" My words were rough and low, but they finally got through to Declan.

His wings flared wide, and he launched himself into the sky, a look of agony on his face.

At least he was getting the gem away from this horde.

My lungs burned as I sucked in air, trying to get the energy to keep up my attack. There were only a few demons between me and that bastard Acius. I had to get to him. It was the only way to call off the onslaught.

Lightning cracked around me as Declan sent bolts of it into the demons that surrounded me. I looked up at him. He was silhouetted against the clouds. Behind him, six enormous winged demons plunged from high above, headed straight toward him.

"Declan!" I shrieked, terror lancing me. "Behind you!"

He turned, but it was too late. They'd performed a coordinated sneak attack, using the clouds for cover. As a horde, they plowed into Declan, plowing him toward the ocean below. They flew with such force that it looked like he'd been hit by a freight train.

Acius cackled, and rage lit a fire inside my chest.

On the horizon, the chopper appeared.

The demons slammed Declan into the ocean so hard that he had to be unconscious. Had to have broken bones. When you hit water while going that fast, it was like crashing into concrete.

Terror charged through me. "No!"

I had to get to him. There were two demons between me and the edge of the platform. I fought like a banshee, hacking through them with my sword.

As Nielson approached, she directed the nose of the chopper at the platform. Bullets sprayed from the guns that I'd never noticed were mounted to the base. She had amazing aim, taking out the demons in quick succession.

I made it to the edge of the platform just as the six winged demons that had attacked Declan burst from the water, flying toward the sky.

Declan was nowhere to be found.

I dove into the sea, swimming as hard as I could to the spot where Declan had gone under. I dove deep, my eyes straining in the dark.

I couldn't see!

The ocean that had once been my love was now my foe. Desperate, I kicked and kicked, my lungs and muscles burning.

But without my sight, it was impossible.

A red glow appeared to my left, a bright light that lit the water around me. Holy fates, it was Wally.

He looked so miserable floating in the middle of the water, but his flame-red eyes glowed so bright that they gave me enough light to see by. He turned his head, shining the glow on the limp form of Declan, drifting twenty feet below me.

I kicked for him, my heart thundering in my head, and grabbed him by the arm. As soon as I started swimming for the surface, Wally disappeared.

Panic surged through me as I made for the air above. Declan had to be unconscious. He had to be.

Not dead.

Not dead.

I couldn't bear it. The world couldn't afford to lose him. I couldn't. I'd waited so long to find someone like him. I hadn't even realized I'd been waiting.

With a gasp, I broke through to the surface. It took all my strength to haul Declan up so his head cleared the water. His neck was limp, and I hoisted him up high enough that he could breathe.

"Come on, breathe!" I searched the oil rig, spotting no motion on the platform. The demons and Acius were gone.

Nielson and her guns had driven them off.

I looked up, following the noise of the chopper. It hovered overhead, the ladder drifting down toward me. Mari and Cass hung out of the chopper door, their concerned faces white in the dark night.

My heart thundered as I kicked to stay afloat, waiting for the ladder to reach me. It drifted close enough, and I grabbed it, grappling with it until I had a good enough grip that I could hang on and also hold on to Declan.

No way in hell I could climb the thing, though. Not with his weight.

Fortunately, Mari and Cass began to haul the ladder up. My arms ached as I clung to the metal slats, wind whipping my hair and threatening to tear me off. Tears poured down my cheeks as I tried to look at Declan's face, but the way I was holding on to him made it impossible.

"Wake up!" I choked on tears, screaming the words.

I couldn't even see if he was breathing. I didn't even know if he was alive.

Pain tore through me, just like the pain I'd felt when I'd thought that Aunt had hurt Mari. Maybe even killed Mari.

Holy shit, was this what love for a man felt like?

This all-encompassing fear for the well-being of another?

It took everything I had to hold on until we were at the top. I pushed on Declan to get him up into the chopper. Mari and Cass struggled with his limp form, finally pulling him inside.

I was reaching for the chopper railing when something grabbed me around the waist. A strong arm yanked me off the ladder and away from the chopper.

Shock tore through me and I screamed.

Mari and Cass looked back from where they'd been tending Declan. Horror flashed on their faces.

Cass threw a fireball, but my captor jerked downward, avoiding the blow.

An icy cold laugh sounded from whoever had captured me.

Acius.

The ether sucked us in, dragging me away from the chopper.

14

THE NEXT MOMENTS PASSED IN A BLUR. THE ETHER SPIT US OUT IN the middle of the woods. I thrashed, trying to break Acius's grip, but pain exploded in my head.

Darkness enveloped me.

When consciousness came, it was in fits and spurts. First there was light. Then the sound of someone pacing. My head ached like it'd been hit with a mallet. Which it might have been.

I blinked, breathing slowly and trying to pretend that I was still unconscious. I needed as much info as I could get about my surroundings before my captors realized I was awake.

My biggest hurdle was that I was chained to a chair. Slowly, I strained against the chains that bound me, but they didn't give.

"I can tell that you're awake." Acius's cold voice reached me.

I groaned, making sure to sound annoyed, and looked up, taking in the natural stone walls around me. We were in a cave somewhere, and the only exit was blocked by an iron gate. Acius leaned his gaunt form against the wall and inspected me.

"You're a real pain in the ass, you know that?" I snapped.

He grinned, an icy smile that made him look like a snake. "I have the gems. All of them."

Shit.

Memories flashed through my head. Declan, plunging into the water. Was he okay?

Please.

Fear gnawed at me, but I shoved it aside. The monsters who'd attacked him had obviously gotten their hands on the gem, which meant that Acius held all the cards.

How should I play this? Could I trick him somehow and steal the gems? I at least needed to figure out what his plan was.

"I'll give you one last chance to join me," he said.

"Hmmm. Maybe. If we discuss terms."

"What terms?" His glare turned suspicious.

"You made a compelling argument last time we spoke. I think I'd like to be a queen." I pursed my lips. "Queen of what, though? That's important."

"Everything." His eyes glinted with avarice. "First, we start with Magic's Bend. It's a perfect base of operations. With all of the residents gone, my loyal followers will have a place. It will be so much easier to operate from the surface, not having to sneak back down into Grimrealm every time we come to the real world."

"And what's my role in all this?" I needed to keep him talking. Any information was good information, and as long as he was talking to me, he wasn't out waking the Great Serpent.

Not to mention, I needed to give my friends as much time as possible to rally the troops. If I failed at this, we'd be going to war.

"With you, I'll have the power to do whatever I want." His eyes turned dreamy. "You can create magic at the drop of a hat. You could rule at my side, overseeing everything. The whole world, created as we wish."

This guy was nuts. Even if I were power hungry, I wasn't actually a ruler in this scenario. I was still his puppet. It was a terrible offer. I'd always thought of myself as a good actress, but pretending to be into this was going to be hard. I needed to play it just right.

"That's compelling." I tilted my head, making sure my expression was as cold as a snake's blood. I could give this guy a run for his money in the ice competition. He'd *never* believe me if I just up and agreed. "But I don't want to be just your minion. I want more than that."

He frowned. "I was afraid you'd say that."

"I'm no one's puppet. But I do like the sound of all that power." I tried to give my voice a bit of longing.

"But you'd join with me? If I gave you what you wanted?"

"I could be convinced." I didn't dare ask him to spare Magic's Bend in exchange. That'd be too obvious.

"Then you won't object to me giving you another dose of my special potion. Just to make sure you're really on my side."

Shit. How should I play this?

That potion didn't just prove my loyalty. It turned me into a minion. I knew it wouldn't work on me, but he didn't know that. If I agreed to it, he'd suspect.

"No," I snapped. "That fogs my mind. I *like* my mind, just the way it is."

"I'd prefer it if it were slave to me." He grinned. "I don't want an equal in all of this. I want a weapon."

Ugh. Dick.

He reached into his pocket and withdrew a vial of potion.

The sight of it made my heart thunder. I cringed backward, trying to make my fear look real. Honestly, it wasn't that hard. I trusted the magic that I'd made—mostly. But we hadn't tested it with *everything.* What if this actually worked?

He approached, his gait relaxed and his eyes excited.

I spit at him. "Bastard."

He chuckled, then bent over me and tilted the vial over my bare arm.

I kicked back, trying to knock my chair over to get out of the way, but he put his foot on my knee, holding me in place. "No, no. None of that now."

He dripped the potion onto my skin. I held my breath, waiting. Waiting.

When the mind-numbing fog didn't come, I nearly slumped in relief. Instead, I stiffened, my eyes going to his. I tried to give my voice some reverence as I murmured, "Master."

He frowned at me.

Shit. Had I done that wrong?

I tried to remember what it felt like when he'd first dosed me with the stuff. An all-encompassing desire to help him had suffused me. I'd have thrown myself into fire for him.

More crazy, then.

"Master, please." I tried to make my eyes desperate. "What do you want of me? I'll do anything."

He stepped back, his frown increasing.

Shit.

"Your eyes should be black," he said.

I raised my brows. "What?"

"If the potion had worked, your eyes would have turned black."

Damn it. "So it wasn't my acting that tipped you off?"

He cursed, low and violently. "What did you do?"

I shrugged. "Exactly what you wanted to use me for, you dick."

"Well, we'll see how you feel once your town is destroyed." Ice hardened his voice.

I bit my lip, wanting to hurl insults at him.

No. Don't piss him off.

I needed to stay conscious. If he knocked me out, I'd lose valuable time.

"No," I begged, the words sour in my mouth. "Please, I couldn't bear it."

An evil grin twisted his features. "Oh, you will. Just sit here and imagine it." He looked at his watch. "In about five hours, when you hear the destruction, you'll know."

Sick bastard. He was doing this to punish me. He liked the idea of me trapped in here, forced to listen to the destruction of my town.

"Please, no." It wasn't hard to make tears come to my eyes. All I had to do was think of what he promised without also imagining myself breaking out of here and stopping him.

He laughed, a sound that sent cold through my veins, then turned and left. He shut the metal gate behind him, turning to look at me. "Just wait for it. Once it's all destroyed, we'll see how you'll feel then. And oh, maybe I'll get your sister, too."

"Bastard!" I screamed.

But he just smiled and walked away.

Panting, I sat in the chair, rage seething through me.

Chill out.

I needed to chill the hell out. I was trapped, but I'd gotten most of what I wanted. Information, and I was still conscious. Now I needed an escape plan.

I tugged at my binding, struggling to get free. The chains were strong. The chair stronger. Both were made of solid iron, too thick for me to break through.

"Wally, pal," I said to the empty cave. "I need some backup."

A moment later, the smoky black cat appeared. His flame red eyes assessed me. *You've gotten yourself into a pickle.*

"Is Declan okay?" Worry still tugged at me.

I haven't seen him.

Shit. "Can you get me out of here?"

He stalked toward me, keenly inspecting the chains. *Definitely. Might not even hurt. But you're going to have to be fast. This metal will heat up quick.*

"Fantastic."

He positioned himself at the back corner of the chair. Heat flared at my back, painful but not burning. It increased, and I winced, tensing my muscles to flee when the chain finally snapped. Sweat dripped down my back as the heat increased, and pain stung my hip where the flame was the hottest.

Go!

I lunged up, fighting the chains and shaking them loose. The chair clattered back behind me.

The door!

A guard appeared in front of the gate, but Wally was fast. He sprinted toward it and blasted a massive fireball. It enveloped the guard, who made a strangled noise before falling. Wally kept up the stream of fire, melting the gate into a puddle that glowed red around the guard's body. The scent of burned flesh made me gag.

I looked at Wally. "Thanks, pal. Acius never saw you coming, did he?"

They never do.

Together, we leapt over the puddle of melted metal and out into the cool night air. Trees soared around me, and I spotted a guard to the right. Not a demon, so most likely a mage. His long black coat flapped around his ankles as he reached for his wrist. I squinted, spotting a comms charm that he had strapped there.

I drew a dagger from the ether and hurled it at him. The blade sank into his shoulder, and he staggered backward. I sprinted for him and leapt onto him, taking him down to the ground.

I yanked the dagger from his shoulder and held it to his throat. "Where will he launch the attack?"

The guard sneered at me. "You're just going to kill me no matter what I do. Doesn't matter if I tell you."

I shrugged. "I could chop off your dick first and feed it to you." I smiled icily. "Actually, I might really enjoy that."

He paled and tried to heave me off him, but I tightened my legs around his chest and squeezed until he couldn't breathe.

"You're sick." The words were forced out of him on a rush as I crushed the air from his lungs.

"Extremely." I pressed the dagger into his throat, drawing a thin line of blood. "Sick and tired of assholes like you propping up a bastard who wants to kill thousands. Now what will it be? Dick or no dick? If there's an afterlife, I hardly think you want to show up with no dick."

He spit at me, and I dodged, barely avoiding the disgusting mass.

"One more of those and I'm slicing it all off," I said.

He grimaced. "Here, all right? Just a mile away, closer to town. There's some kind of barrier protecting the city so he can't raise the serpent in there."

Relief flashed through me. That meant Jude had managed to get the barrier created. It'd buy us time. And his words jived with what Acius had said. *Five hours hence, and I'd be able to hear it.*

"Where is here? Where are we?" There were a lot of woods surrounding Magic's Bend. Precise location would save me time in getting picked up.

"Northwest of Magic's Bend, near Honeycomb Falls. They're a hundred yards behind us."

"When's the attack?" I demanded, just for good measure, even though I was pretty sure Acius had been telling the truth.

"Dawn."

I had no idea what time it was, but this guy definitely didn't seem like he was lying.

"How many fighters does he have?"

"More than you can fight."

I pressed the blade deeper. "Seriously, how many?"

"A hundred."

Shit. A hundred demons and mages from his cult, plus the serpent. We had to get to him before he tried to raise it, because once he did, it was over for us.

I sliced the mage's neck and dodged the spray of blood, then climbed off him and pressed my comms charm at my throat.

"Mari?"

"Aeri!" Her relieved voice came through.

"I've been trying to reach you. No answer. Where are you?"

"I was unconscious for a while. Is Declan okay?"

"He's okay. *Where are you*?"

Relief flashed through me, making my muscles turn to water. "I'll meet you at Honeycomb Falls in two minutes."

"Be there in a sec."

I looked at Wally. "Thanks, pal."

He inclined his head.

I sprinted through the woods, heading in the direction that the guard had indicated. Soon, I heard the water. I spotted it a moment later, catching Mari just as she appeared. She spun around, relief flashing on her face when her eyes met mine.

"Oh, thank fates!" She raced forward and flung her arms around me.

I hugged her tight, and the ether sucked us in as she transported us back to our place. We arrived in the middle of the living room in the main house, a space we used only for formal events as Aerdeca and Mordaca. It was totally full, bustling with people.

My gaze went unerringly to Declan. How I knew where he'd be standing, I had no idea. But it was like he wore a homing beacon.

I raced toward him, my heart lighting up like it was the Fourth of July. Relief filled his eys, and he caught me up in his arms, pulling me close.

"Thank fates." His voice was rough against my neck, his grip almost too tight. "When I woke and you were gone, I thought I'd lose my mind."

"I thought I'd lost you." My throat tightened and tears prickled. "I thought I'd lost you."

"You didn't." He pulled back, his eyes on me.

"I think I might love you," I said at the exact same time he said, "I don't want to live in a world without you by my side."

The words jumbled up together, a mess of emotion.

I didn't know what to expect when I'd blurted the words—just that I wanted to say them. Just in case I never got another chance.

But what he'd said...

"Really?" I asked.

He nodded. "And I'm fairly certain that means I love you back."

"But this was crazy fast."

"It was." He tightened his grip around my waist. "But all I needed was to wake up and think you were dead to realize how I felt."

"Me too." Holy fates, I loved him.

He loved me.

And we had the battle of a lifetime to fight.

All around, people bustled as they got ready for the battle. More and more arrived every second, crushing in on us as the room filled.

There was no time for this.

Every second counted.

I pulled back. "We'll continue this later. Right now, we need to stop Acius. He's gone to deploy the stone and raise the Great Serpent."

Mari appeared at my side, her timing perfect. "Ready?"

I turned to her. "Ready. What's our situation?"

Jude appeared a moment later, Bree and Ana at her side. The two Dragon Gods, along with their sister Rowan, were some of the most powerful supernaturals at the Undercover Protectorate. I was glad they were here. I had to assume that Rowan was off on extremely important business, or she'd be here too.

"Thank you for coming," I said.

Mari and I had always helped the Dragon Gods and the Protectorate in the past because we'd wanted to. But now, it was paying off in spades.

Two of the three FireSouls showed up a half moment later. Nix and Del looked dirty and exhausted from their other mission.

"Cass gave us the update," Del said.

"She's out running recon now with Aidan, searching for their forces from the sky."

"Has she found anything yet?" I asked.

"Not yet," Del said.

Behind them, I spotted their men—Ares and Roarke—along with Cade and Lachlan, who'd come with Bree and Ana.

Lastly, Connor and Claire joined us. Connor had his usual potion bag slung over his shoulder, and Claire wore her fighting leathers and a grim expression.

We had the whole force, now. We'd need them all.

"We managed to get a shield in place around the town," Jude said. "But it won't last forever."

"Acius has figured that out," I said. "According to one of his guards, he's going to deploy the stones at the edge of town, near Honeycomb Falls."

"Perfect." Grim satisfaction rang in Mari's voice. "We needed a location. We can tell Cass and Aidan to focus their aerial search in that part of the forest."

"He has a troop of at least a hundred demons and mages protecting him while he deploys the stones." I scanned the room. We had at least eighty, a collection of fighters from the Protectorate and Magic's Bend. Nothing to sneeze at.

"I'm going to fly ahead and join the recon effort." Declan met my gaze. "I'll let you know when I've spotted them."

"I'll go with him," Nix said. "More eyes on the ground is good. We need to find them ASAP."

"Us too." Bree gestured to her and Ana. "We'll find them before you reach the edge of town and let you know exactly where to go."

"Once we have a location, our ground forces will hold off the demons who are protecting Acius. He should be trying to perform the spell that will raise the Great Serpent. Mari and I, along with the rest of the airborne unit, will go straight for Acius and try to stop him before he raises the Great Serpent."

"And if he does raise the serpent?" Jude asked.

"We try to kill it."

Try being the operative word. We'd all heard the stories about how they were impossible to kill. Only a Thunderbird had ever accomplished it in the past, and there were none of those left. At least, none that we could convince to help us.

"I'll spread word through the ground troops," Jude said. "When we arrive at the front, they'll know what to do."

Everyone murmured their assent and split up.

I gave Declan a quick, hard kiss.

He caught my eye. "Be careful, okay?"

"You too. And come get me once you've found Acius. I'll need a drop-off past the front line."

He nodded and gave me one last kiss. I leaned into it, savoring the last moment before battle. When he departed, he was joined by Roarke, who could also fly. That gave us a force of six searching the area around Honeycomb Falls.

After everyone had been briefed, we set out as a huge force, piling into cars and trucks to head to the edge of town. A massive, armored vehicle covered in spikes and adorned with fighting platforms at the front and back rolled slowly by. It was driven by a woman with bright platinum hair, with two dark-haired men riding front and back. Caro, Ali, and Haris—three members of the Protectorate. Ali and Haris reached down, giving a hand to other Protectorate members, who piled on.

It was Ana and Bree's buggy, as they called it. Normally one of them would drive, but they were airborne right now.

Ali spotted me. "Come on! You can have the front."

I looked at Mari, and she nodded. We strode toward the buggy and climbed onto the front platform, getting a front-row view as we drove to the edge of town. Our long caravan passed hundreds of cars heading in the other direction.

"Evacuations started hours ago," Mari said. "As soon as we lost the stone, the mayor started moving people out."

I nodded, setting my jaw and keeping my gaze forward, avoiding the weary faces of those who passed by. Guilt stuck like a knife in my gut. If I'd just beaten Acius to either of the two stones, we wouldn't even have this problem.

"I want to kill that bastard," I muttered.

Mari squeezed my hand. "You're going to have to beat me to him."

"Together?"

She met my gaze. "Together."

15

AIR RECON LOCATED ACIUS'S FORCES, AND OUR CARAVAN TURNED to follow their directions. My heart thundered loud and slow as I tried to calm myself before the battle to come. As we neared the edge of town, I noticed the gleaming shield rising up from the ground and arching over it as a great dome. It flickered a pale blue.

Magic prickled across my skin as we rolled through it. In the distance, I could see the demons milling through the trees. They were joined by a horde of red-cloaked cult members. The two groups formed a line between us and Acius, though I couldn't quite see him past their bodies.

Our forces climbed out of vehicles and assembled in a line. We stayed on the front platform of the buggy, which would drive right into the battle, and I turned to look at the mass of warriors. Some I recognized, others I didn't. But I appreciated all of them, more than I'd ever be able to express.

Deep in my gut, though, I had a feeling that it would come down to just me and Acius. It was going to take everything I had to defeat him—I just hoped I had enough.

The demons roared.

The battle began.

We charged. As the buggy plowed toward the front line, Cass flew toward us. She was in her griffon form, her massive lion's body strong and powerful as her eagle's head turned toward Mari. She swooped down, and Mari climbed onto her back. Declan followed, dipping down and grabbing me up.

I held on tight as he flew us high over the fighters. They clashed, our mages against their demons and red cloaks. Fireballs flew and magic exploded on the air. The buggy plowed over a dozen demons as the fighters on the platforms fired magic and weapons into the horde.

Del, her blue phantom form flashing, wielded her sword against a group of red-cloaked cult members. They threw blasts of strange-colored magic at her, but she was too fast, dodging it before it could collide with her form.

On the other side of the battle line, Jude cracked her electric whip, taking out a demon twice her size as her black braids swung around her head. Ares, the vampire, moved so fast that I could barely see him, but demon blood flew when he passed the monsters by.

The cult members were putting up a good fight, but their red robes slowed their movements.

Idiots.

I scanned the forest below for Acius. Tree cover was sparse here, and I spotted him in the middle of the clearing. He'd burned a triangle into the ground, and each of the three gems was placed at a point. He stood in the middle, his hands raised over his head as he chanted words I didn't recognize.

Our airborne fighters attacked the protective barrier that surrounded him. I could barely see it, but I could see Bree's lightning crashing against the dome and fizzling out. Aidan, also in griffon form, slammed his huge body into it, unable to break through.

"We can't get through!" Declan shouted. He threw a lightning bolt at it, but it bounced off, the same as Bree's had done.

Shit.

Magic swelled from Acius as he chanted, the spell barreling toward completion.

We had to get through that barrier.

But how?

We had no idea what the spell was made of, so no way to know what would break it.

I had to try to nullify it.

"Drop me at the edge!" I shouted. "In a quiet spot."

My friends continued their assault on the barrier as Declan did as I requested. I leapt out of his arms and raced to the barrier, my gaze glued to Acius. The bastard had a look of joy on his face that made me want to gut him.

How far along was he?

The ground rumbled under my feet, as if to answer my question.

Fear chilled my skin.

Shit.

I hovered my hands over the barrier, trying to get a feel for the magic. It prickled and burned, enough to indicate that this was probably going to hurt.

A lot.

I called upon the nullification power that slumbered, letting it rise inside me. When it filled my chest, I pressed my hands to the glowing barrier. Electric energy sparked fiercely against my hands, and I cried out. Pain tore through me.

"It's an extension of his electric magic," I gritted out, feeding my gift into the barrier.

"Stop." Declan's voice was agonized. Watching me do this but not being able to help must have been tearing him apart.

"I can't."

He growled, but said nothing else. He knew I couldn't stop.

Pain weakened my muscles as I forced my magic into the barrier, desperately trying to break it down. Mari joined me, leaping off Cass's back and racing to my side.

She grabbed my shoulder with one hand and thrust the other into the barrier, grunting in pain. She didn't have nullification magic, but she was an amplifier, one who was able to increase the magic that another used.

I sucked in a deep breath, panic fluttering in my chest as I worked. Mari's hand dug into my shoulder as she amplified my power, and the barrier began to fizzle. It broke away around our hands, our power streaking outward and weakening the magical dome that protected Acius.

I pushed hard against the barrier, hoping I could shove my way through, but it was still too strong.

"Almost there," I muttered, forcing more power into the dome. My legs weakened and my breath grew short.

Mari's face paled, and her eyes dimmed.

"This bastard is strong." She set her jaw, and her magic flared brighter.

We were nearly through.

Acius's magic surged, and he laughed. The three gems that surrounded him grew bright, glowing like stars going supernova.

Magic exploded through the air, throwing me backward. I landed hard on the ground, the wind knocked from me. The earth shook violently, and I scrambled upright, barely able to keep my footing.

Next to me, Mari rose, her face pale. She grabbed onto me as the ground tore apart in front of us. An enormous serpent rose from the earth, at least ten stories tall and twenty feet in diameter. It knocked over a dozen massive pine trees with one swing of its huge head.

On the other side of the serpent, the battle between mages

and demons halted, every single fighter staring in horrified awe at the giant snake.

Fear like I'd never known flashed through me, freezing me solid.

Acius's cold, triumphant laugh snapped me back to attention.

He was going to drive it toward the town.

In the sky, Bree sent a massive bolt of lightning at the snake. Declan joined her, their bolts surging through the monster as it swayed like a cobra.

The creature didn't even jerk.

More lightning shot up from the ground, every single lightning mage directing the full force of their attack at the beast. In their griffon forms, Cass and Aidan dove for the creature's eyes, their front claws extended to gouge. The creature jerked its head away so fast that they missed.

Hundreds of fireballs flew at the monster. Declan's heavenly fire was the only thing that even made the creature wince, but there was no way he could conjure enough of it. The monster began to move, slithering forward, headed toward Magic's Bend. Nearly everyone in our army leveled the full might of their attack, but they barely slowed the beast.

"Oh fates," Mari murmured. "We can't fight it."

A horrible, wonderful, terrifying idea flashed in my mind's eye. "Not in this form."

There was only one thing that had ever defeated a Great Serpent before.

Mari looked at me. "What do you mean?"

A blast of electric energy plowed into me, slamming me back into the ground. Pain crippled me, and I gasped, staring blankly at the trees above.

"Aeri!" Mari screamed.

Out of the corner of my eye, I spotted her racing toward me, drawing a wooden shield from the ether. In the distance, Acius stalked toward us. On the other side of him, our forces retreated, following the Great Serpent.

Mari crouched in front of me, her shield raised to block us both.

"Get up!" she shouted.

I dragged myself to my feet, every inch of me aching. "Cover me."

"On it." She shook as another bolt of electricity hit her shield.

Acius stalked closer, his eyes on us. "You can't stop it!"

His shout sent a bolt of rage through me. The Great Serpent slithered away, mowing over enormous trees as it headed for the city. How long would the barrier hold?

Not long. Not against a monster as strong and impervious as that one.

Mari slammed the shield into the ground to create a barrier and drew her bow from the ether. She fired at Acius, screaming, "Coward! You hide behind your serpent and your lightning, but you're nothing!"

Rage lit on his face. His hands glowed as he powered up another blast.

I knelt on the ground, thrusting away my worry for Mari in favor of envisioning a new power for myself. Quickly, I sliced my veins, going deeper and bigger than ever before. I had to bleed. Quickly.

Any concerns I'd had about hiding my true nature were pointless now. This was more important.

White blood poured onto the leaves around me, flowing quickly as my head began to spin. I forced my magic out along with it, envisioning gaining a new power. New strength. New gifts. Something that maybe wasn't even real, but I wanted it to be.

It was insane, what I was trying to do.

I did it anyway.

In the sky, Declan battled alongside the other airborne fighters, leveling their attacks against the serpent. Lightning crashed and griffons dived. Mari held off Acius with her bow and arrow, finally drawing a sword when he got too close. She made sure to stand between him and me, giving me time to work.

Though the forces were retreating, trying to keep up with the serpent as it approached Magic's Bend, I was out in the open. Anyone could look over here and see what I was doing.

What I was.

But hell, they wouldn't need to. If this worked, they'd all know something was up with me. There was absolutely no turning back after this. No hiding.

The world would know what I was.

Weakness tugged at me as I worked, my blood and magic flowing out as I imagined what I could become. My vision was nearly black by the time Acius reached Mari. She was staggering from his repeated electric hits.

Terror for her filled me. I forced the last of my power out of my body, and finally, magic snapped in the air. It changed, becoming something more. Something so powerful that when it flowed back into me, fear lit a fire in my chest.

Fear for myself.

Fear *of* myself.

The magic filled up my soul, surging into me with such force that I gasped and slammed backward onto the ground. My back arched and my vision went totally dark. I could feel death reaching for me.

This was different than any other magic I'd ever created. It took so much from me that I could feel the cold grip of the reaper.

Until everything changed. Power twisted around my body,

pain and pleasure all at once. The magic of the dragon rose in my blood, fiercer than ever. I was becoming what I was meant to be—my final transition as a Dragon Blood, made possible by the magic rising inside me.

My muscles changed, my bones grew. My eyes snapped open, and the forest looked different. Clearer. I could see individual leaves high above me in the trees. An ant crawled on one leaf, oblivious to the chaos below.

Strength surged through my muscles, dragging me back from the precipice of death.

I burst toward the sky, a triumphant shriek tearing from my beak.

Only once I looked down did I realize how enormous I must be. My wingspan was forty feet. Maybe fifty. I flapped my wings, and thunder cracked on the air.

It had worked.

I was a Thunderbird. The only creature that could defeat the Great Serpent.

Mari was on her knees beneath me, but Acius was on his, too. He was studded with arrows and sliced with cuts, struggling to stand.

Holy shit, Mari had almost taken him out.

I dived, beak first, headed right for my prey. Something animalistic inside me rejoiced at the idea that I would taste Acius's blood soon.

He looked up as I approached, fear flashing on his face. I shrieked at him, enjoying the terror in his eyes, then picked him up in my beak and chomped down so hard that his legs fell to the ground. The rest of him was inside my mouth, but I spit him out, the bloodlust faded.

I gave Mari a quick look.

She was down, but she managed to give me a thumbs-up. "Go."

I whirled on the wind, heading for the Great Serpent. The wind blew through my feathers as I soared over the trees. The sound of cracking thunder and shouts drew me to the battle.

I approached as the Great Serpent reached the magical barrier. The creature slammed its head against the dome, making cracks shoot through the surface. Cries sounded from the warriors down below. They hurled magic at the snake, which slowed it, but couldn't defeat it. Whatever demons and red cloaks were there ran for it, trying to escape now that Acius was dead.

I swooped down from behind, aiming right for the base of the serpent's head. I dug my claws into the flesh below the skull, then flapped my wings, thunder cracking on the air. I heaved with all my might, trying to drag the serpent away from the city.

But it was too damned heavy. I only got the beast a few feet into the air before it slammed to the ground only a few dozen yards from the barrier. It turned, rearing its head to strike up at me. Emerald green eyes glinted as its mouth opened wide, revealing enormous fangs.

For the first time since I'd transformed, fear flashed through me.

This thing could kill me.

It lunged upward, trying to sink its fangs into me. I flew back, and the creature's fangs sank into the edge of my wing. I tore away, pain flaring. The wound was minor, thank fates.

I darted out of the way of the creature's second blow, then whirled back in and smashed one of my wings onto its head. Thunder boomed, and the Great Serpent's eyes shook.

I whirled on a circle again, hitting the beast a second time. All around, the fighting ceased. My friends didn't dare shoot magic at the serpent for fear that it would hit me.

On my third approach, the serpent lunged upward, aiming for my chest. I darted right, my wings carrying me out of harm's way. I whirled on the air and dived again, heading for the serpent's head.

My claws raked across the face as the creature lunged for me. The fangs sank into my wing—deeper into the flesh this time—and the monster crashed its head to the ground, taking me with it.

The enormous weight of the beast crushed me to the dirt. I could feel its muscles tensing up on top of me, probably to wind themselves around me and crush me to death.

I flapped my wings, slamming them hard against the ground. Thunder cracked, vibrating through the serpent. The fangs dislodged from my wing, and I kicked up with my claws again, shoving the serpent off of me and leaving him with deep puncture wounds in its belly.

While the serpent regained its composure, I struggled to my feet, then launched myself back into the air. Pain surged through my wings and some of my ribs felt broken from the snake's weight, but I could still maneuver.

I circled the serpent, who rose to its full height, eyes trained on me. Carefully, I inspected the creature, looking for the best place to land a killing blow. I couldn't afford to be caught by it again—the force of its attack could cripple me.

My eyes narrowed. I just needed to get to the sensitive spot beneath the serpent's neck. It was one of the narrowest parts of the body, and there had to be arteries there. But I needed to avoid the fangs.

As if he'd heard my thoughts, Declan swooped in front of me, flying toward the serpent. As he neared the head, he flew upward, then shot his lightning down at the serpent's head. The beast looked up to follow his movement and the lightning.

I took my chance, darting forward and approaching with my claws positioned in front of me. I sank them into the serpent's neck. The creature hissed and thrashed, and I dug deep, tearing through muscles and tendons.

I flapped my wings, creating thunder that made the serpent shake. With all of my might, I jerked away from the monster, tearing out its throat. Blood poured, and the beast collapsed.

I flew out of the way, darting toward the safety of the sky. When I was out of range of the serpent, I turned to inspect the damage.

The creature lay collapsed on the ground outside of the barrier that protected Magic's Bend. Its blood flowed like a river, pooling thickly around the broken form. Dark magic began to sizzle up from the body, reeking of sulfur and decay. Within minutes, the Great Serpent disappeared, the dark magic that had created the monster fading away into the dawn.

The demons and the red cloaks were all gone, drifted into the woods or transported away. We would probably never see them again, and if we did, they were nothing without Acius.

All around, our fighters stood. They were bloodied and broken, exhausted and dirty, but I saw no collapsed bodies. Though there were grievous injuries, I thought we might have gotten away without causalities.

Every single one of them watched me with wide eyes. Even Wally looked impressed, his little jaw dropped to reveal two white fangs.

I debated landing and showing myself. I had no idea if people had seen me transform. By the time I'd fully shifted, they'd been farther away, busy battling the serpent. They might not even realize that the Thunderbird was me.

I shrieked, then spun on the air, flying away from the crowd. I didn't want credit and I didn't want to be seen. More than that, I needed to check on Mari.

I flew back to where I'd left her, flying down to the clearing where I'd transformed. She lay on the leaves, staring at the sky.

Fear chilled my blood as I landed. Shifting back to my human form took only a thought, and I fell to my knees at her side.

"Mari!" I shook her shoulder. She'd been more hurt than I'd realized.

She turned her head to look toward me. "I feel like shit."

Declan landed next to me. His wings folded in, and he leaned over Mari.

I turned to him. "Heal her!"

"I'm on it." His voice was soothing as he pressed his hands to Mari's shoulders.

Heavenly light glowed from his palms, and the pain that twisted Mari's features faded. The lines between her brows smoothed out and her lips unpinched.

When he was done, he removed his hands, and she sat up, looking beat to hell. "Thanks."

I looked at them both, all the adrenaline and fear of the last few days coursing through my body.

We'd survived. All three of us.

Magic's Bend had survived.

I threw my arms around them and hugged them tightly, squeezing them to me. They hugged me back, and I swore I could feel the disbelief in their grips.

Thank fates we'd made it.

As the adrenaline flowed out of me on a rush, I realized how drained I was. Turning into the Thunderbird had taken everything I'd had. Darkness rose up to take me.

EPILOGUE

THE NEXT DAY, AFTER I'D RETURNED TO CONSCIOUSNESS AND everything had settled down, we did the only reasonable thing we could.

We threw a party.

This one was at our house, which was odd under normal circumstances. We'd thrown parties for Darklaners before—but they were always intended to be a way to consolidate power and increase our status in the neighborhood. We'd never thrown a genuine party meant to celebrate, and we'd definitely never invited our friends or people from outside of Darklane.

This time, though, we did. Because we really had something to celebrate. Despite some truly horrific injuries, there'd been no casualties on our side. The big bad was defeated.

Life went on.

And we partied.

Mari and I sat on a long couch that was pressed against the wall in our large rectangular living room. We each wore our normal city clothes, and thank fates for that. I needed a break from the fight wear and constant battle. At the present moment, my martini was cold and my ivory dress was silky smooth. And I was *clean.*

No more sweat or blood or seawater. It was heaven.

I sipped my icy martini, watching the crowd mingle.

"Things have really changed," Mari murmured.

"They have indeed." I spotted Nix, Cass, and Del on the makeshift dance floor that had popped up in the middle of the room.

A live band was playing in the corner—mostly Fae, since they were so good with music—and the FireSouls were getting down on the dance floor. All three of them had sustained grievous injuries in the battle, but they'd healed up well enough.

I squeezed Mari's hand. "I can't believe no one has said anything about me."

She met my gaze. "They may not realize that the Thunderbird was you."

"I hope so. But I've got a feeling that's not the case. At least a few people could guess."

"The FireSouls." Mari nodded. "They know enough to guess. But they'll protect your secret."

That, I could count on.

"Honestly, even if the town *did* know, I don't think they'd ever breathe a word. Not after you saved us all."

"It was a team effort."

"But *you* were the Thunderbird," Mari said.

"It was wild. I could feel the dragon magic rising inside me in a way it never had before." The memory of turning into the massive bird still blew my mind. It had been incredible. Terrifying, but amazing. The amount of power it had taken had been immense. It'd almost killed me. I wouldn't be using that gift much in the future—I wouldn't be able to.

But it'd been amazing all the same. Partially because I'd felt like I was truly in control. My signature had definitely changed as a result.

"You've got your signature under control, though," Mari said. "I can barely sense that you're different."

"It was the fear," I said. "I was so afraid of the new powers I could create that it was impossible to control them. They were in charge. But I'm not afraid anymore."

"Good." She sipped her Manhattan and studied the crowd. "I always had faith you could."

"Thanks." I squeezed her hand.

We sat in the kind of comfortable silence that is characteristic of the best relationships. As I watched the people mingle, I thought of the secret chamber below our house. Of the pool that connected us to the Council of Demon Slayers.

"Not a single one of them has any idea what's below this room," I said. "After all we've been through, so much of our life is still a secret."

"I prefer it that way," Mari said. "I don't mind sharing with some—like with the FireSouls—but this works for us."

"Agreed." I preferred life in the shadows. We'd come into the light just enough to add some brightness, but this was enough.

From across the room, I spotted Declan. He stood a full head taller than most of the crowd around him, so he was easy to spot. His gaze met mine, and he smiled.

"So, you two are official, huh?" Mari asked.

"Yeah." I hadn't mentioned it to her—hadn't had the time—but she could tell. Sisters were like that. "It's crazy. It happened so fast. But it just works."

"Yeah." She gave me a quick side hug, then stood. "I'm happy for you."

I smiled. "Thanks."

"And now, I'm going to go refill my drink." She raised her nearly full Manhattan.

"You don't need another drink yet."

"But you need a free spot on the couch." She grinned and whirled away, disappearing through the crowd.

Declan appeared at my side a moment later. He'd cut quickly through the crush of bodies, moving gracefully despite his size.

I gestured to the seat next to me and smiled.

He sat, then leaned over and pressed his lips to mine. I fell into the kiss, swept away by his touch. Warmth flared within me, followed by competing feelings of comfort and desire.

Finally, he pulled away. "I've been waiting to kiss you all day."

I met his dark gaze. "Likewise."

"Nice party you've got going here."

"I like to think so."

"Can you spare some time later tonight?"

"Oh? For what?" I grinned at him.

"A little trip."

I tilted my head. "To where?"

"Well, you've just defeated one of the world's greatest evil masterminds. Not to mention a mythical snake of murderous proportions. I think you could use a break. Let's take a little trip. Just the two of us. Somewhere relaxing. The beach in Greece?"

"That sounds like it's even better than a date."

"I can't guarantee a demon won't randomly pop up, but I've cleared my schedule. I'm not going after any bounties, and I bet the Council of Demon Slayers would give you a couple days off."

"I can sneak away." Mari would let me know if shit hit the fan, anyway. I looked for her in the crowd, spotting her with Connor and Claire.

Everything was perfect.

The town was safe, my friends were having fun. Even Wally was enjoying the crowd.

I'd saved the day.

Yeah, I deserved a break with my handsome fallen angel.

I looked at him. "Let's get the hell out of here."

He grinned and pulled me to my feet. We made our escape through the back door, and I couldn't help but feel like I was walking toward a fuller life. One in which I was no longer afraid of what I was. I'd come full circle to my childhood—creating magic when I needed it—but I was in control now. And that made all the difference.

THANK YOU FOR READING!

I hope you enjoyed reading this book as much as I enjoyed writing it. Reviews are *so* helpful to authors. I really appreciate all reviews, both positive and negative. If you want to leave one, you can do so on Amazon or GoodReads.

If you'd like to learn a little more about the FireSouls, you can join my mailing list at www.linseyhall.com/subscribe to get a free ebook copy of *Hidden Magic*, a story of their early adventures. Turn the page for an excerpt.

Mari's series is coming later this summer, so keep your eyes peeled!

EXCERPT OF HIDDEN MAGIC

Jungle, Southeast Asia

Five years before the events in Ancient Magic

"How much are we being paid for this job again?" I glanced at the dudes filling the bar. It was a motley crowd of supernaturals, many of whom looked shifty as hell.

"Not nearly enough for one as dangerous as this." Del frowned at the man across the bar, who was giving her his best sexy face. There was a lot of eyebrow movement happening. "Is he having a seizure?"

"Looks like it." Nix grinned. "Though I gotta say, I wasn't expecting this. We're basically in a tree, for magic's sake. In the middle of the jungle! Where are all these dudes coming from?"

"According to my info, there's a mining operation near here. Though I'd say we're more *under* a tree than *in* a tree."

"I'm with Cass," Del said. "Under, not in."

"Fair enough," Nix said.

We were deep in Southeast Asia, in a bar that had long ago been reclaimed by the jungle. A massive fig tree had grown over and around the ancient building, its huge roots strangling the stone walls. It was straight out of a fairy tale.

Monks had once lived here, but a few supernaturals of indeterminate species had gotten ahold of it and turned it into a watering hole for the local supernaturals. We were meeting our contact here, but he was late.

"Hey, pretty lady." A smarmy voice sounded from my left. "What are you?"

I turned to face the guy who was giving me the up and down, his gaze roving from my tank top to my shorts. He wasn't Clarence, our local contact. And if he meant "what kind of supernatural are you?" I sure as hell wouldn't be answering. That could get me killed.

"Not interested is what I am," I said.

"Aww, that's no way to treat a guy." He grabbed my hip, rubbed his thumb up and down.

I smacked his hand away, tempted to throat-punch him. It was my favorite move, but I didn't want to start a fight before Clarence got here. Didn't want to piss off our boss.

The man raised his hands. "Hey, hey. No need to get feisty. You three sisters?"

I glanced at Nix and Del, at their dark hair that was so different from my red. We were all about twenty, but we looked nothing alike. And while we might call ourselves sisters—*deirfiúr* in our native Irish—this idiot didn't know that.

"Go away." I had no patience for dirt bags who touched me without asking. "Run along and flirt with your hand, because that's all the action you'll be getting tonight."

His face turned a mottled red, and he raised a fist. His magic welled, the scent of rotten fruit overwhelming.

He thought he was going to smack me? Or use his magic against me?

Ha.

I lashed out, punching him in the throat. His eyes bulged and he gagged. I kneed him in the crotch, grinning when he keeled over.

"Hey!" A burly man with a beard lunged for us, his buddy beside him following. "That's no way—"

"To treat a guy?" I finished for him as I kicked out at him. My tall, heavy boots collided with his chest, sending him flying backward. I never used my magic—didn't want to go to jail and didn't want to blow things up—but I sure as hell could fight.

His friend raised his hand and sent a blast of wind at us. It threw me backward, sending me skidding across the floor.

By the time I'd scrambled to my feet, a brawl had broken out in the bar. Fists flew left and right, with a bit of magic thrown in. Nothing bad enough to ruin the bar, like jets of flame, because no one wanted to destroy the only watering hole for a hundred miles, but enough that it lit up the air with varying magical signatures.

Nix conjured a baseball bat and swung it at a burly guy who charged her, while Del teleported behind a horned demon and smashed a chair over his head. I'd always been jealous of Del's ability to sneak up on people like that.

All in all, it was turning into a good evening. A fight between supernaturals was fun.

"Enough!" the bartender bellowed. "Or no more beer!"

The patrons quieted immediately. Fights might be fun, but they weren't worth losing beer over.

I glared at the jerk who'd started it. There was no way I'd take the blame, even though I'd thrown the first punch. He should have known better.

The bartender gave me a look and I shrugged, hiking a thumb at the jerk who'd touched me. "He shoulda kept his hands to himself."

"Fair enough," the bartender said.

I nodded and turned to find Nix and Del. They'd grabbed our beers and were putting them on a table in the corner. I went to join them.

We were a team. Sisters by choice, ever since we'd woken in a field at fifteen with no memories other than those that said we were FireSouls on the run from someone who had hurt us. Who was hunting us.

Our biggest goal, even bigger than getting out from under our current boss's thumb, was to save enough money to buy concealment charms that would hide us from the monster who hunted us. He was just a shadowy memory, but it was enough to keep us running.

"Where is Clarence, anyway?" I pulled my damp tank top away from my sweaty skin. The jungle was damned hot. We couldn't break into the temple until Clarence gave us the information we needed to get past the guard at the front. And we didn't need to spend too much longer in this bar.

Del glanced at her watch, her blue eyes flashing with annoyance. "He's twenty minutes late. Old Man Bastard said he should be here at eight."

Old Man Bastard—OMB for short—was our boss. His name said it all. Del, Nix, and I were FireSouls, the most despised species of supernatural because we could steal other magical being's powers if we killed them. We'd never done that, of course, but OMB didn't care. He'd figured out our secret when we were too young to hide it effectively and had been blackmailing us to work for him ever since.

It'd been four years of finding and stealing treasure on his behalf. Treasure hunting was our other talent, a gift from the dragon with whom legend said we shared a soul. No one had seen a dragon in centuries, so I wasn't sure if the legend was even true, but dragons were covetous, so it made sense they had a knack for finding treasure.

"What are we after again?" Nix asked.

"A pair of obsidian daggers," Del said. "Nice ones."

"And how much is this job worth?" Nix repeated my earlier question. Money was always on our minds. It was our only chance at buying our freedom, but OMB didn't pay us enough for it to be feasible anytime soon. We kept meticulous track of our earnings and saved like misers anyway.

"A thousand each."

"Damn, that's pathetic." I slouched back in my chair and stared up at the ceiling, too bummed about our crappy pay to even be impressed by the stonework and vines above my head.

"Hey, pretty ladies." The oily voice made my skin crawl. We just couldn't get a break in here. I looked up to see Clarence, our contact.

Clarence was a tall man, slender as a vine, and had the slicked back hair and pencil-thin mustache of a 1940s movie star. Unfortunately, it didn't work on him. Probably because his stare was like a lizard's. He was more Gomez Addams than Clark Gable. I'd bet anything that he liked working for OMB.

"Hey, Clarence," I said. "Pull up a seat and tell us how to get into the temple."

Clarence slid into a chair, his movement eerily snakelike. I shivered and scooted my chair away, bumping into Del. The scent of her magic flared, a clean hit of fresh laundry, as she no doubt suppressed her instinct to transport away from Clarence. If I had her gift of teleportation, I'd have to repress it as well.

"How about a drink first?" Clarence said.

Del growled, but Nix interjected, her voice almost nice. She had the most self control out of the three of us. "No can do, Clarence. You know... Mr. Oribis"—her voice tripped on the name, probably because she wanted to call him OMB—"wants the daggers soon. Maybe next time, though."

"Next time." Clarence shook his head like he didn't believe

her. He might be a snake, but he was a clever one. His chest puffed up a bit. "You know I'm the only one who knows how to get into the temple. How to get into any of the places in this jungle."

"And we're so grateful you're meeting with us. Mr. Oribis is so grateful." Nix dug into her pocket and pulled out the crumpled envelope that contained Clarence's pay. We'd counted it and found—unsurprisingly—that it was more than ours combined, even though all he had to do was chat with us for two minutes. I'd wanted to scream when I'd seen it.

Clarence's gaze snapped to the money. "All right, all right."

Apparently his need to be flattered went out the window when cash was in front of his face. Couldn't blame him, though. I was the same way.

"So, what are we up against?" I asked.

The temple containing the daggers had been built by supernaturals over a thousand years ago. Like other temples of its kind, it was magically protected. Clarence's intel would save us a ton of time and damage to the temple if we could get around the enchantments rather than breaking through them.

"Dvarapala. A big one."

"A gatekeeper?" I'd seen one of the giant, stone monster statues at another temple before.

"Yep." He nodded slowly. "Impossible to get through. The temple's as big as the Titanic—hidden from humans, of course—but no one's been inside in centuries, they say."

Hidden from humans was a given. They had no idea supernaturals existed, and we wanted to keep it that way.

"So how'd you figure out the way in?" Del asked. "And why *haven't* you gone in? Bet there's lots of stuff you could fence in there. Temples are usually full of treasure."

"A bit of pertinent research told me how to get in. And I'd

rather sell the entrance information and save my hide. It won't be easy to get past the booby traps in there."

Hide? Snakeskin, more like. Though he had a point. I didn't think he'd last long trying to get through a temple on his own.

"So? Spill it," I said, anxious to get going.

He leaned in, and the overpowering scent of cologne and sweat hit me. I grimaced, held my breath, then leaned forward to hear his whispers.

As soon as Clarence walked away, the communications charms around my neck vibrated. I jumped, then groaned. Only one person had access to this charm.

I shoved the small package Clarence had given me into my short's pocket and pressed my fingertips to the comms charm, igniting its magic.

"Hello, Mr. Oribis." I swallowed my bile at having to be polite.

"Girls," he grumbled.

Nix made a gagging face. We hated when he called us girls.

"Change of plans. You need to go to the temple tonight."

"What? But it's dark. We're going tomorrow." He never changed the plans on us. This was weird.

"I need the daggers sooner. Go tonight."

My mind raced. "The jungle is more dangerous in the dark. We'll do it if you pay us more."

"Twice the usual," Del said.

A tinny laugh echoed from the charm. "Pay *you* more? You're lucky I pay you at all."

I gritted my teeth and said, "But we've been working for you for four years without a raise."

"And you'll be working for me for four more years. And four

after that. And four after that." Annoyance lurked in his tone. So did his low opinion of us.

Del's and Nix's brows crinkled in distress. We'd always suspected that OMB wasn't planning to let us buy our freedom, but he'd dangled that carrot in front of us. What he'd just said made that seem like a big fat lie, though. One we could add to the many others he'd told us.

An urge to rebel, to stand up to the bully who controlled our lives, seethed in my chest.

"No," I said. "You treat us like crap, and I'm sick of it. Pay us fairly."

"I treat you like *crap,* as you so eloquently put it, because that is exactly what you are. *FireSouls.*" He spit the last word, imbuing it with so much venom I thought it might poison me.

I flinched, frantically glancing around to see if anyone in the bar had heard what he'd called us. Fortunately, they were all distracted. That didn't stop my heart from thundering in my ears as rage replaced the fear. I opened my mouth to shout at him, but snapped it shut. I was too afraid of pissing him off.

"Get it by dawn," he barked. "Or I'm turning one of you in to the Order of the Magica. Prison will be the least of your worries. They might just execute you."

I gasped. "You wouldn't." Our government hunted and imprisoned—or destroyed—FireSouls.

"Oh, I would. And I'd enjoy it. The three of you have been more trouble than you're worth. You're getting cocky, thinking you have a say in things like this. Get the daggers by dawn, or one of you ends up in the hands of the Order."

My skin chilled, and the floor felt like it had dropped out from under me. He was serious.

"Fine." I bit off the end of the word, barely keeping my voice from shaking. "We'll do it tonight. Del will transport them to you as soon as we have them."

"Excellent." Satisfaction rang in his tone, and my skin crawled. "Don't disappoint me, or you know what will happen."

The magic in the charm died. He'd broken the connection.

I collapsed back against the chair. In times like these, I wished I had it in me to kill. Sure, I offed demons when they came at me on our jobs, but that was easy because they didn't actually die. Killing their earthly bodies just sent them back to their hell.

But I couldn't kill another supernatural. Not even OMB. It might get us out of this lifetime of servitude, but I didn't have it in me. And what if I failed? I was too afraid of his rage—and the consequences—if I didn't succeed.

"Shit, shit, shit." Nix's green eyes were stark in her pale face. "He means it."

"Yeah." Del's voice shook. "We need to get those daggers."

"Now," I said.

"I wish I could just conjure a forgery," Nix said. "I really don't want to go out into the jungle tonight. Getting past the Dvarapala in the dark will suck."

Nix was a conjurer, able to create almost anything using just her magic. Massive or complex things, like airplanes or guns, were outside of her ability, but a couple of daggers wouldn't be hard.

Trouble was, they were a magical artifact, enchanted with the ability to return to whoever had thrown them. Like boomerangs. Though Nix could conjure the daggers, we couldn't enchant them.

"We need to go. We only have six hours until dawn." I grabbed my short swords from the table and stood, shoving them into the holsters strapped to my back.

A hush descended over the crowded bar.

I stiffened, but the sound of the staticky TV in the corner made me relax. They weren't interested in me. Just the news, which was probably being routed through a dozen techno-witches to get this far into the jungle.

The grave voice of the female reporter echoed through the quiet bar. "The FireSoul was apprehended outside of his apartment in Magic's Bend, Oregon. He is currently in the custody of the Order of the Magica, and his trial is scheduled for tomorrow morning. My sources report that execution is possible."

I stifled a crazed laugh. Perfect timing. Just what we needed to hear after OMB's threat. A reminder of what would happen if he turned us into the Order of the Magica. The hush that had descended over the previously rowdy crowd—the kind of hush you get at the scene of a big accident—indicated what an interesting freaking topic this was. FireSouls were the bogeymen. *I* was the bogeyman, even though I didn't use my powers. But as long as no one found out, we were safe.

My gaze darted to Del and Nix. They nodded toward the door. It was definitely time to go.

As the newscaster turned her report toward something more boring and the crowd got rowdy again, we threaded our way between the tiny tables and chairs.

I shoved the heavy wooden door open and sucked in a breath of sticky jungle air, relieved to be out of the bar. Night creatures screeched, and moonlight filtered through the trees above. The jungle would be a nice place if it weren't full of things that wanted to kill us.

"We're never escaping him, are we?" Nix said softly.

"We will." Somehow. Someday. "Let's just deal with this for now."

We found our motorcycles, which were parked in the lot with a dozen other identical ones. They were hulking beasts with massive, all-terrain tires meant for the jungle floor. We'd done a lot of work in Southeast Asia this year, and these were our favored forms of transportation in this part of the world.

Del could transport us, but it was better if she saved her power. It wasn't infinite, though it did regenerate. But we'd learned a long time ago to save Del's power for our escape. Nothing worse than being trapped in a temple with pissed off guardians and a few tripped booby traps.

We'd scouted out the location of the temple earlier that day, so we knew where to go.

I swung my leg over Secretariat—I liked to name my vehicles —and kicked the clutch. The engine roared to life. Nix and Del followed, and we peeled out of the lot, leaving the dingy yellow light of the bar behind.

Our headlights illuminated the dirt road as we sped through the night. Huge fig trees dotted the path on either side, their twisted trunks and roots forming an eerie corridor. Elephant-ear sized leaves swayed in the wind, a dark emerald that gleamed in the light.

Jungle animals howled, and enormous lightning bugs flitted along the path. They were too big to be regular bugs, so they were most likely some kind of fairy, but I wasn't going to stop to investigate. There were dangerous creatures in the jungle at night—one of the reasons we hadn't wanted to go now—and in our world, fairies could be considered dangerous.

Especially if you called them lightning bugs.

A roar sounded in the distance, echoing through the jungle and making the leaves rustle on either side as small animals scurried for safety.

The roar came again, only closer.

Then another, and another.

"Oh shit," I muttered. This was bad.

~~~

Join my mailing list at www.linseyhall.com/subscribe and get a free ebook copy of *Hidden Magic.*
~~~

AUTHOR'S NOTE

Thank you for reading *Dragon Rise!* If you have read any of my other books, you might be familiar with the fact that I like to include historical places and mythological elements. I always discuss them in the author's note.

One of the most obvious historical elements was the Templar castle. It is based upon the castle by the same name, *Krak des Chevaliers,* which is located near the Syrian coast. The Order of the Knights Hospitaller were given the castle in 1142, after which they immediately began rebuilding it. At the height of it's occupation, it held 2,000 troops. In 1271 AD, the Knights Hospitaller lost the castle after a 36 day siege.

Baphomet is an interesting figure in historical documents. No one really knows if the Templars actually worshipped Baphomet, who is described as being a severed head, a cat, or a head with three faces, and historians have discussed the topic for decades. The name appears primarily in 1307, when Philip IV of France began his own crusade against the Templars. He wanted to destroy their order, and thus he had many of them arrested and charged with various religious crimes. In order to get the torture to stop, many of the Templars did confess to the crimes they were accused of, among which was the worship of Baphomet (which many modern scholars agree is an Old French corruption of the name Muhammad). Under torture, different Templars described Baphomet in different ways—as the severed head, the cat, or the head with three faces. I can only imagine that they invented these things under duress in order to get the torture to stop, but there is not a lot of information about it.

I wasn't a huge fan of this torturous version of history, and I've never met a three headed cat I didn't like, so I cherry picked the best bits to create my own version. Which is nowhere near the truth, what little we actually know of it.

Probably my historical favorite part of the story is that of Sam McGee, the frozen man in the steampunk town. He is based upon a poem called The Cremation of Sam McGee by Robert Service. The humorous poem was published in 1907 and is a real doozy. I came across it while recording the shipwreck of the *A.J. Goddard,* a steamboat that has featured in several of my books.

The poem was inspired by the Klondike Gold Rush in the Yukon Territory and takes place partially on the shores of Lake Laberge, where the *A.J. Goddard* wrecked. It tells the story of Sam McGee, a gold prospector who froze to death up in the Yukon. His last request was that he be cremated and not buried in the cold ground, and his friend followed through with his last wishes.

However, it's really hard to cremate someone in the depths of the frozen north, so his friend had to carry Sam's body around until the found a boiler from a ship wrecked on the shores of Lake Laberge. The boat was called the *Alice May*, not the *A.J. Goddard* (a body never would have fit in the *A.J. Goddard's* little boiler anyhow), and it was the perfect place for Sam's friend to finish the grisly dead. So he stuck Sam's body in there and fulfilled his friend's dying wish.

In my version of the tale, Sam lives and moves to the steampunk town, but he has a distinct fondness for climbing into boilers and his only true wish is to be warm again (which Aeri will definitely help him with).

I think that's it for the history and mythology in *Dragon Rise* —at least the big things. I hope you enjoyed the book and will come back for more of the FireSouls and Dragon Gods's worlds.

ACKNOWLEDGMENTS

Thank you, Ben, for everything. There would be no books without you.

Thank you to Jena O'Connor and Lindsey Loucks for your excellent editing. The book is immensely better because of you! Thank you Eleonora, Richard, and Aisha for you helpful comments about typos.

Thank you to Orina Kafe for the beautiful cover art.

ABOUT LINSEY

Before becoming a writer, Linsey Hall was a nautical archaeologist who studied shipwrecks from Hawaii and the Yukon to the UK and the Mediterranean. She credits fantasy and historical romances with her love of history and her career as an archaeologist. After a decade of tromping around the globe in search of old bits of stuff that people left lying about, she settled down and started penning her own romance novels. Her Dragon's Gift series draws upon her love of history and the paranormal elements that she can't help but include.

COPYRIGHT

Published by Bonnie Doon Press LLC

Linsey@LinseyHall.com
www.LinseyHall.com
https://www.facebook.com/LinseyHallAuthor

Made in the USA
San Bernardino, CA
20 June 2020